8/26/05
Christ
Enjoy The

Best, H. Mertins
aka Helen Struble

FIRST LIGHT

BY

H&M MERTINS

authorHOUSE™

1663 LIBERTY DRIVE, SUITE 200
BLOOMINGTON, INDIANA 47403
(800) 839-8640
WWW.AUTHORHOUSE.COM

First published by AuthorHouse 03/24/05

ISBN: 1-4208-3043-0 (sc)

Library of Congress Control Number: 2005901111

Printed in the United States of America
Bloomington, Indiana

This book is printed on acid-free paper.

FIRST LIGHT

The first light eradicates the last bit of darkness. It pierces the ending shadows to turn the night's blackness into the gray of dawn. Does it eliminate the evil thoughts that darkness caresses? Evil is as evil does.

Let there be light and light there was. The beautiful albatross, soaring about on wide splayed wings, is not concerned with the countryside of the Highlands with its firths and its glens. Concerns himself not of what he views and the cacophony of sounds he hears. The sounds of merriment, and the death toll chimes below go unnoticed. His peripheral eye has no reason to see castles nestled in the ancient groves of trees or fortresses that look out to the sea, unaware of smoke emitting from newly lit firesides, or rivers that flow south. Cares less about love and hate! And evil doings. But they do travail.

This wild bird decides it is time to eat. Sand oysters would suit him nicely. On his return flight over twisted rocks that run to the sea, he thinks only of survival… his basic need… in the first light.

CHAPTER ONE

First Light.

They stole away in the first light of the rising moon. It was just a simple, arranged escape, happening just a few hours from the time he had placed his gold ring upon her finger, an act that would bond them together for eternity, until death do they part. They fled the medieval castle grounds in secrecy, just the two lovers and enough strong men to safely man the ship.

The sloop, "Victory," stood rigged and ready in the harbor. She has logged many a trip through both sunny skies and gales. Her massive bow will slice through the temperamental currents of the Knell River with ease, navigating gracefully with each ebb and flow. Sails were up and billowing. The water, choppy.

Brightly lit orange fire torches send golden sparks into the night sky as if in celebration. The full round moon, peeking through the wispy gray clouds high above, nods farewell to the setting sun. The stars are coming out to play and the ship's captain will measure their distance from the horizon with his dependable sextant as he sets his course, and will stay the course to his final destination, Fortress Lockmoor.

The honored passengers stand arm in arm on the ship's bow, engrossed in each other and in their own private thoughts. There are stars in the heavens and stars in Fiona's eyes as well. Inside her brain, she heard the smiling sounds of fiddles, bagpipes, and tin whistles, and inside her mind's eye, she saw the lively dancers stepping highly-- the brief memory of all that gaiety now fading much too quickly.

In route, Steward impulsively tosses his new bride's wedding wreath of orchard blossoms into the river's deep and dark swirling water in a gesture of freedom, saying laughingly to Fiona, "Blossoms for the sea god's golden locks... we are free to love... as we please... whenever we please."

Within the hour, the lovers reach the destination of their honeymoon, called mi na meala, a common term in the highlands of Eire. The boat drops anchor port side of the sturdy dock made of oaken pilings and red boulders. Fortress Lockmoor, at the mouth of the Knell River, stands sequestered away among towering black trees, secluded from the inquisitive eyes of friend or foe. A backdrop of rolling hills surrounds the sturdy fortress. Glens, woodlands, lush and rolling green meadows, sparsely dotted with blue bells and goldenrod and covered with copious patches of briar bush and brambles, add to this remote setting.

This mighty stone fortress had belonged to Fiona, the bride. She brought this strategically located and valuable piece of land to the wedding table as her dowry in exchange for love from her newly wed husband. Now Steward of Castle Baine belongs to her. Standing guard at the fortress is a garrison of worthy men, who keep the fires lit, the cupboards stocked, and the ale plentiful.

The Bride and Groom.

Fiona and Steward, alone at last, had slipped away from their wedding feast held in the Great Hall of Castle Baine. The blithe couple was more than happy to leave behind their betrothal ceremony, an incredible well-planned and orchestrated celebration indeed. The day would go down in greatness. Masterful minstrels sang songs of love and bravery, and jaunty jugglers aptly provided much of the lively and humorous entertainment and gaiety.

On her wedding day, the bride felt as if she looked like a vision of purity in her dark blue velvet-wedding gown. The chosen practice of the time was for the bride to wear blue as the color was thought to portray the true love of the bride for the groom. The low-cut bodice of her gown was tastefully styled, showing just enough cleavage to keep Steward watching her every move throughout the day with sexual curiosity.

Over her long and shiny straight brown hair, she had worn a colorful ribboned wreath of green ivy entwined with white apple blossoms. If asked, most of the guests at the wedding would agree that Fiona was a beautiful woman, second only to Steward's mother, Lady Kyla, who simply looked and acted the role of a perfect golden goddess at all times. She has never been seen being involved in any wrong doing… always flawless in every word, deed, and action she presented to the public.

And today had been no exception to Kyla's aura of perfection. All eyes were riveted on her when she made her appearance, proud and regal, at the wedding feast in the Great Hall. Lady Kyla wisely chose to wear an elaborate dark green velvet gown with a taut bodice and tightly fitted sleeves that displayed more than fifty golden buttons on each arm. The gown's long flowing skirt was richly trimmed in gold and silver brocade that moved with careless elegance with each tiny step she took… a lovely sight to behold.

Atop her long blond hair, Lady Kyla wore a fashionable high pointed hat, a barbette, with an attached veil of white chiffon that cascaded over her shoulders and down her back, giving her a most regal appearance. A matching ornate hyacinth necklace complemented her lovely look of splendor. Upon simple observation, a guest could note that Kyla's sparking piece of jewelry far outshone the small single-stoned Chrysoprase necklace that Fiona had chosen to wear as a true symbol of her love for Steward.

The elaborate three course bridal meal was directed with great aplomb. Kyla had ordered the servants to prepare three freshly cooked courses of soup, roasted quail, turtledoves and partridge, roasted cheeses, silvered calves' heads, and a peacock, cooked and reassembled with its feathers in place, be served to the wedding guests. She also provided each diner in the Great Hall with an uniquely made personal silver spoon to aid them in devouring the special lavish feast, but most chose to eat with their fingers.

Kyla was overly delighted when the invited noblemen and honored guests cheered and laughed heartedly as the piece de resistance, an intricate sotelty, a huge, life-like dessert sculptured in marzipan, replicating the scene of six blackbirds baked in a pie, was brought in piping hot from the kitchen. A work of art!

"Luckily, when the pie was opened, none of the birds began to sing," mused Kyla.

Then, in the midst of the frivolity and merrymaking, Kyla's visage turned ice cold; her mood suddenly flashed from gay to somber and gray as visceral thoughts flood her mind.

"I will truly miss my first born son, my dear Steward, who has turned to the arms of a younger woman for solace."

Mi Na Meala.

With the day of feasting, merriment, and many blessings behind them, Fiona and Steward are quite content to be safe at Lockmoor. They plan to spend all their private moments making love and romping in the hay bed, so to speak.

For their honeymoon gift, they had been given jugs of mead made from the goodly hazel-bush and fermented honey. This wedding brew is believed to hold special meaning. If the bride and groom share the unique golden liquor for one full moon, they are guaranteed powers of virility and fertility as their bodies unite in lovemaking. And drink the potent golden mead they do, raising their pewter goblets high and toasting their blissful unity.

"I truly need to be united with you," Fiona whispers. "You're a wild thing… in need of taming!"

Steward teased… "And I am impatient to make love to you."

"Come, follow me," commands Fiona, as she laughingly leads Steward to the fortress' main bedchamber.

Upon entering the room, Steward notes row upon row of lighted, glowing candles, their flames dancing, eerily casting shadows that flicker and waltz on the walls and across the white bed linens and pillows. Flowers from the meadow have been placed around the large room, giving off the sweet welcoming aroma of juniper and laurel. Amongst the blossoms is a single pure white rose, positioned there by Fiona herself... a symbol of her virginity.

In the dim light, Steward instantly reaches out for Fiona and caresses her bare shoulders. He kisses her hair and then her soft full lips. His hands move to her wedding dress, but he has little to no patience as he struggles with the small fasteners of the gown. The lacings kindle his sexual desires. He literally claws at removing the garment. Fiona helps by ridding her body of all its material restrictions and moves quickly and nimbly beneath the fur covers and heavy blankets of the great double bed.

Within moments, Steward is in bed beside her, he puts his arms around her, and pulled her in, touching and kissing every bend and curve of her body. He trusts his maleness into her quickly, again and again, and establishes a rhythm that Fiona greedily welcomes inside her. As their two bodies rise and fall in unison, Fiona begins to feel a forceful sensation rising within her. Before she is able to release this pulsating feeling in a scream of pleasure, Steward peaks with fulfillment and collapses heavily onto her body.

Lying there in the night, Fiona feels the need for love stirring within her. She caresses her thighs, which are tingling with warmth, and feels a strong hot sensation centered inside her loins. She is about to caress herself further when Steward grabs her wrists and forces her hands high above her head. Lowering his head, he crushed his mouth to hers. His hot tongue of lust moves to lick at her breasts, encircling her nipples again and again. The wet heat of her surrounds him. His lips, his tongue, his hands, the scent of her, he wanted all of that.

Fiona begs in delight, "Enter me... now." No sooner had she given the command, when suddenly, Steward slid hard inside her.

"Stay with me," he whispered.

His motions begin slowly, and within seconds he reaches a wild and frantic pace. This time, Fiona is brought to complete satisfaction... now, as well as the next time, and the next.

In time, sleep engulfs the bride and the groom.

Second Light.

At second light, clamorous sounds of frantic fuss and hubbub hits like a tidal wave; guards race toward the bridal bedchamber, vociferously pushing and shoving one another in their haste to deliver the deadly news. Deafening knocks on the door follow, awakening the lovers from their love dreams and shattering their peacefulness. Raucous shouting of "Master Steward! Master Steward!" can be heard, men's voices echo discordantly from the cold stone passageway.

Steward answers the wild commotion with poised caution, and steps into the hallway. The next sound Fiona hears is Steward's screaming and shrieking like a banshee-- piercing the night-- wild high pitched mournful sounds of anguish that rise and fall like the waves of the Irish Sea. These doleful cries seem to flow out from the inner most depths of Steward's soul.

"NO! NO! NO! Who could have done this heinous act? Who would trespass onto the castle ground... my land? Who so dared kill my family?" wails Steward.

Enemy in the Night.

Fiona soon learns that while they were on their lovemaking sojourn, the enemy had come in the night to Castle Baine. Steward listened in horror as the guards hastily inform him of Castle Baine's night of devastation and fire... flames leaping from dark to dark. His mother, Lady Kyla, and his half brother, Edmud, discovered in a bedchamber of the East tower, had been slaughtered... their bodies flamed. The room was torched, becoming a dark black empty hole... infamy... death... at first light.

Had it been the barbaric intruders plan to kill Steward and me as well? Had we escaped a cruel and deadly fate while filling our need for love?

Of the castle guards standing watch, some had been savagely beheaded, and it was feared that the others had been run off... or perhaps chose to jump from the steep castle battlements into the raging Knell River below to escape the high leaping flames, a fate more deadly than facing the blistering blaze. No one is thought to have survived the savage fire in the east tower. Kyla is dead. Edmud is dead. Many guards... dead... or missing.

And what of the servants? Had they not heard the cries of anguish? They, too, became part of the macabre riddle. Had this hellish group of workers compensated for their daily hard struggles and labors by partying too hardy, as was their practice? Could it be surmised that most had been foolishly drunk that evening... either from finishing off every last drop of wine or liquor remaining in the guests' wedding goblets? Or, perhaps someone had deceivingly filled each servant's very own lead cup to the brim with ale or whiskey... a risky combination... intending to knock each one out... rendering all useless.

These drunken scalawags and sots now lay unconscious on the kitchen tables of the castle... while their family awaits to see if any will awaken in the next day or two. Who knows if one of these befuddled servants will remember the virulent fire... or even remember their own name!

How could this devastating pillage have happened? What is to be the fate of Castle Baine?

The Torment.

Fiona hears her new husband roaming and ranting through the fortress calling out his mother's name, the words echoing off the giant walls.

"Kyla, Kyla, this cannot be," moans Steward, his torment unbearable.

But his wife Fiona cannot help silence his suffering nor ease his heartache, try as she may. She prays to the river goddess Coventina to help him bare the grief of his mother's cruel death and find comfort for his bleeding heart.

Fiona is alarmed. Steward's reactions to death are not only bizarre, but also morbidly self-destructive. He sits moodily and despondent. He carves at his body with a sharpened knife, injecting pain. His blood flows. Such actions remind Fiona of the tale of penance once told to her by her grandparents: In ages past, self flagellation was practiced by the highland's peasants and nobles during the time of the Black Death. Men would publicly whip their upper bodies into raw bleeding pulp with leather cat-o-nine tails in an effort to drive out sin. As it was believed that the Black Death only infected the unholy and the impure… a man, free of sin, could survive the curse of the plague.

"Is Steward purging himself of some past sin?" Fiona wonders.

Steward turns to drink. It eases his suffering, slowly at first, but then he continues well into the night… night after night. He is often blind drunk on wine and mead. He stumbles. He falls… but he is never again falling into their bed. Fiona spends sleepless nights thinking of him; she sorely longs for his loving touch and begs for his sensual embrace, just once more.

Silence is taking over their marriage.

CHAPTER TWO

Desperate for Help.

Fiona must find Una. She is her only hope at this time of great need. She decides to leave in the first light of day to search out this life long friend who she had teasingly called the "witch wizard of the swamp" during their earlier years of pretending together as children... dancing in the forest... playing in the fields... chanting songs to the wind.

In Fiona's eyes, Una is a beautifully tan skinned girl with a gypsy mane of long black hair that cascades loosely down her back until she ties it back tightly with a thin band of black cloth. She has eyes that are dark yet filled with fire... eyes that can see right through you! So too does she possess "the second sight," the clairvoyance to predict the future and to know the past... the ability to see into the dark of night, knowing each sound and sight by heart... truly intelligent and intuitive.

Her benevolent smile, though quick, is marked by a space between her two large white front teeth, giving her a sense of severity... or is it a mark of the Coventry? One would question her startling appearance further if he could see the wild pictures etched on her slim arms. They resemble a dragon's heads, tinted purple by the juice of the black cohosh berries gathered from the forest floor. Her look is unique and mysterious, a look designed by Una herself.

But the most remarkable thing about Una is her knowledge of alchemy. She possesses the power to work miracles with herbs, seeds, and all forest floras; she is truly dangerously magical. Fiona knows that Una will choose the best herbs for Steward. A potion to halt his wild dreams... his self-mutilation; or perhaps she will create a balm to ease his aching pain-filled body... and re-ignite his passion for love.

Into the Forest.

An icy rain is falling as Fiona begins her desperate search for Una. The sky above is dark and ominous, the weather, chilly. A mist is on the rise.

"I must carry out my plans to get in touch with Una today, weather be hanged. She is my trusted confidant, the only friend who can help me!" declares Fiona, her heart resonating with hope.

She enters the wet green of the weald and tries desperately to recall the exact way to Una's camp by the river. She had traveled the rocky path often as young lass that the pathway she must take eases its way back into her mind. Both man and time have altered the once familiar woodlands. The steady falling rain makes the trip seem darker and gloomier than she remembered. The trek was long and arduous—a journey not to be undertaken lightly. At times, she looses her footing as she dodges between the prickly briars and the many pointed pine needles that have fallen from the tall dark woods. She pushed deeper into the woods. The growth turned thick, and sticker bushes snagged at her ankles. Often, her feet slide on the slippery slope, and she finds it necessary to steady herself, grabbing hold of twisted branches to keep from falling. The hems of her skirt and petticoats are now wet from traipsing through the wild overgrown ferns.

The cold steady rain continues to spatter mist from the green canopy of tall trees. The caw of birds can be heard overhead, sharp, stirring up the scent of pine. She pushed a low hanging branch out of the way and maneuvers slowly but directly to a clearing by a rapidly flowing current of the Knell.

Nearing her destination, Fiona is gripped by the feeling of being spied upon from within the dark foliage. She remains calm. She senses that her every step is being counted.

Noah must be nigh. I feel his eyes upon me.

Gratefulness engulfs her as she realizes that she is nearing Una's remote camp. Entering the glade, she sees smoke rising wistfully from a small hut's chimney. The thatched hut, built of wooden logs and stacked stones, is a most welcomed sight. Her heart races with anticipation. At that moment, Noah steps in front of her, lightly challenging her… as in the past.

"So where is Missy going in such a hurry?" he asks, a quiet smile crossing his lips.

Fiona, catching her breath, replies. "Oh Noah, thank goodness! I thought that was you guiding me to Una. I am so relieved that I could find this place again. I was working from my childhood memory of this path I often traversed in the past."

Pausing for a moment, Fiona blurts out, "Oh Noah, I need Una's help so desperately."

"Go inside, Missy," Noah commands goodheartedly. "Your trusted friend awaits you. You are safe now!"

Una, the Swamp Witch.

As she entered cozy scented hut, Fiona's senses are greeted by the sight of colorful plants and flowers hanging upside down to dry from the cabin's rafters; a myriad of apothecary jars, filled with herbs, roots, and powders, cluster together in the far corners. A sweet earthly fragrance rises from the bubbling cauldron at the fireplace, filling the room with the warmth of welcome. But, the melodious sound of Una's convivial voice gives the most sensory welcome of all!

"Fiona, you're here! How wonderful!"

Una rushes to Fiona, and throws her arms tightly around her, greeting her dear friend with a strong and friendly embrace.

"I knew you were coming. Look at you! You have such an aura of dread surrounding you."

Upon hearing her lovely soothing voice, Fiona falls into Una's arms and weeps.

"There, there, good friend. You come seeking help for another. Together we can help him."

Fiona narrates the story of Steward through short gasps for breath and quiet sobs. She feels so relieved when the tale is over that she falls into Una's arms again, and softly whispers, "Help me. Please!"

"This I can do," said Una. "But first, I need you to get your thoughts clear; I need you to find peace."

She gently picks up Fiona's right hand and caresses it with both of her own. She tenderly follows the lifeline that extends from Fiona's palm to her wrist. Lost in deep concentration, Una hesitates, momentarily, before she speaks.

"You need to be wise for your journey ahead, Fiona. Many things will challenge you… you need your strength… you must think rightly. Do not let your fatuous emotions blind your reasoning as to what is going on around you. You are in more danger than your husband be."

Una pauses now, and looking at Fiona with great concern, continues. "I see that a seed in growing within you. You must take care of this small one who will come to you. This will not be an easy task. I will give you something that will keep you healthy and will ward off all evil doers."

A gasp tumbled from Fiona's lips. "Don't tell me about me, tell me about Steward! He needs your help."

"Hush, my old and dear friend," said Una. "The gods direct me to warn you that you do not truly know Steward. He seems to be in agony. But is his pain real? Think of this upon your return home."

"Help Steward," pleads Fiona, a knot caught in her throat.

"Yes, I will give you special herbs and balm for his self inflicted wounds. But I will give you more, something for you." Una's soft words sound like soothing magic… secret whispers.

"Now, follow my directives diligently. Take this milk thistle, turmeric, and bilberry. Grind them together. Take the mixture of these three each morning during your awaiting time."

Una adds salient advice in stronger tones. "The potion will help you to keeps your wits about you as you learn things you were not meant to hear or see. Protect your thoughts and you will come to understand the confusion around you. Know full well that everyone has a secret, a dirty little secret, they don't want you... or anyone to uncover. Evil and danger surround you. Identify truths and falsehoods. Only then will you be free from harm."

Fiona sits stunned, her hand covering her mouth in shock and amazement. She fights a rising trepidation within her and murmurs in confusion, "What are you saying?"

Una's response is most direct. "What I am telling you is true. Be ever watchful. You have been duped. Lies and untruths encircle you; they are powerful, dangerous. Be brave and know that the gods will protect you. You are a chosen one."

Una's warnings recommence. "Sharpen your wits... take care of those around you... but trust no one... a deadly mistake."

Handing a jar of green colored salve to Fiona, she proceeds with her remunerations. "Take this balm to ease your husband's pain... but so too, learn the true reason he assaults himself physically. Be wary... perhaps his pain is deeply rooted in his mind. You are blinded by your own thoughts of love. Not wise. Loving someone leaves you vulnerable to betrayal. Be perceptive. Search out the root of other's actions, other's wicked ways."

Fiona is both alarmed and frightened by this warning of existing evil. She clutches her shaking body and slumps over in quiet disbelief.

Una puts her loving arms around her friend. "Be strong Fiona. You have been warned, my dear friend. I pray that you have strength and enlightenment. You must and will survive the darkness that shrouds you."

Being Guided Back.

When Fiona leaves Una's small camp guided by Noah, the weather is starting to clear. The highland wind swirls and storm clouds depart. The rain was just spitting now… both chilling and damp. She feels safe and secure having Noah guide her return to the fortress, through eerie fells and forest, a straight path as the raven flies. Noah carries her bundle of powerful elixirs and plant supplies in a sack upon his broad back.

Taking the lead, Noah says, "We must not dilly dally, Missy."

He had been her guide copious times in the past, when, as a young girl, she had come to play with her childhood friend, the mystic of the forest, and he eagerly assumes this role again. Fiona had known him almost as long as she had known Una, and she was well aware that he had her best interest at heart. They spoke little. Words were not necessary. Just a nod of the head would suffice. It was their method of silent communication.

Heading home in the light drizzle, the tale told about Noah, this one armed strong man, runs though her mind. Story has it that Una's kind mother, Suda the Sorceress, had saved Noah's life when he was a lad of 12 or so. A starving child then, Noah was caught stealing gold coins from the marketplace.

He was hauled before the local chieftains' self-appointed judge and jury, and convicted of the crime. Guilty! Noah's sentence was most harsh. The jury decided to have the punishment fit the crime... he is to have his hand severed from his body.

The only person to show Noah any help or compassion is Una's mother. Left to die in the town square, Suda takes the boy to her hut by the river. She gives him herbs made from the powerful plants found in the deep woods to ease his pain, but she cannot dull his hate and desire for revenge. She bathes his bleeding stump in a mixture of yarrow, aloe salve, and spider webs; she binds his mutilated arm in leather; she eliminates his fear and comforts his anguish when he cries out to the darkness.

Each night, by the light of the fire, Suda performs a wild, ritual dance in the hope of relieving Noah's torment and suffering. She can be heard chanting to the gods, "Nar laga Dias do lamh" (May the gods not weaken your arms' strength).

In time, Noah recovers. He learns how to survive in the forest. Once a young marksman with a bow and arrow, he becomes a champion with the skills of a warrior; he can wield an ax with a deadly aim. He pledges his allegiance to Suda and her young daughter Una, white witches both, hermitics of the woods, the magic makers.

Fiona thanks the gods that this brutally handsome man became her protector as well, her guardian and friend. She feels safe… having nary a fear… as she travels on her route to and from Una's safe, secluded camp.

The Magical Cure.

Following Una's directions, Fiona knots barley straw around a rock and tosses it into the Knell River to take away Steward's pain. She sprinkles angelica in the four inside corners of his bedchamber to exorcise all evil spirits from his room; she feeds her husband the herbs to ease his mind, and tenderly spreads the balm over his carved skin to help his agony. Miraculously, Una's special elixirs work within a fortnight. Inexplicable magic!

Steward soon feels physically well; his libido activates. He urgently needs to have his sexual needs satisfied. He begins by making lustful, coercing demands upon Fiona, commenting, "As a man, as a husband, I have needs… that must be met."

Gratefully, Fiona welcomes him back into their marriage chamber. Steward anxiously begins fondling her body, gently.

In the midst of their passionate lovemaking, Fiona whispers her secret… she is carrying the seed of their first child.

Steward's angry reaction catches Fiona off guard. He is livid. He shouts into her face, "No! Do not tell me that! Do not speak of a child conceived on that evil and mournful night of my mother's death. I can not forgive you! You are carrying a demon seed. Until you are rid of the child within you, I will never come to your bed again. You are cursed. Can you not understand that?"

Fiona's face is white with alarm at the words she is hearing. "Steward... please..." she begs.

"I will not touch your body... ever again. You no longer pleasure me."

His words pierce her heart with a razor-sharp pain, as if run through by a warrior's lance. "But I love you," Fiona weeps as she struggles to understand. "I need you ... and you cannot survive without my love... nor I without yours."

"But my lovely bride, I need you not. I will not lack for love, fornication... and manly pleasure. As you are unholy to be with, I will find my satisfaction elsewhere as is my male given right," the foul tempered Steward adamantly retorts.

Fiona pleads on. "Please do not do this to me, my husband."

"Never interfere in my thoughts or my deeds," Steward snaps, his voice becoming nearly a hiss.

Silence. Morbid silence. Its uncomfortable tone filled her with agony and anguish. Would his travesty of words invade her entire life at Lockmoor?

CHAPTER THREE

Silence.

Two people – battling for supremacy, so self-centered that they are quite oblivious to the horrors that encircle them. They stand in the mist of raging battles, castle versus castle, and bother themselves with their own pleasures and contentment, turn love into hate. Hate – the winner! Sadness – the friend. When did it start? When will it end? This fencing, using one's heart as a foil… the man, quite oblivious to his handsomeness, the woman, uncaring about her beauty. Dark – deep dark eyes avert the mating of the golden amber eyes of the wife, eyes that well up in tears, without provocation. Embers of the once burning fire of life smolder and die. Sneaking away like a thief in the night. No footsteps to trace.

Their life at the fortress becomes one of total loveless silence… Each one turned to his personal means of endurance to withstand the pain. Their own private cobwebbed world. Fiona, quietly, on tiptoe, advanced to the music room of the fortress. A place she often journeyed to when feeling alone and unloved. Out of harms way.

The harp, her harp, with its strings of various contrivances, was still taut, much to her delight. The strings, set in an open frame, bravely wore colors of pink and shades of blue. The proud face of a pretty angel stood boldly at the helm. Gingerly, she laid the instrument upon her shoulder. Dust scattered as she began to pluck the stings with nimble fingers. She played a musical sound, the musical call of the bird—the raven's note. Playing the semibreve, or whole notes with authority, the eight notes or quaver and the half note or minim- with gusto, Fiona is transported on the wings of sound to her youth and happy carefree days—under the tutelage of her music instructor. Escape from the now on lofty wings of sound.

Can one return to one's happy childhood? One wishes. Music. Poetry set into motion and rhythm. Music—life's remedy.

Steward has a different remedy. He turns to the bottle for comfort and warmth. He starts drinking wine. He glares at Fiona in stony hate. Their late day meal is as cold and silent as the catacombs of early Christians. Her efforts at communication are thwarted at every turn. At the end of the meal, Steward greedily swallows his goblet of wine, and rides off into the night.

Fiona has overheard, from the incessantly gossiping servants, that Steward has made cavorting with the local young trollops and prostitutes of the town a habit. He does not return to the fortress till the sun is on the rise. She listens. He staggers up the stairs, noisily, habitually inebriated.

He has stopped his every attempt at lovemaking. He no longer comes to her bed, choosing to sleep off his drunkenness in a separate bedchamber at the end of the dark hallway. There are no tender touching and no soft words spoken between them, just as he warned. Fiona was alone—more alone than she ever could have imagined... alone in her dungeon of depression.

"How has our love died so rapidly?" she queried. "Had Steward lied to me from the very beginning? Had he not even loved me then… as he does not love me now?"

In her soul, Fiona senses that her husband's unfaithful ways will bring sin into their household, yet her loins ache excitedly… feverishly… for him and his maleness.

The guard on the turret announces to the drawbridge tender, "All is well"… quite unaware that doom, masked in blackness, has already entered the gates of the mighty fortress.

Confrontations Persist.

There is beauty all around when there is love at home, sings the bard. Love does not abide here in the fortress. Gloom does. Doom does. Clouds are gray and lifeless. During the day the sunshine fails in its efforts to polish each blade of grass – and at nighttime, the melancholy moon gives off a sad light. It appears a side order of murk has been dished up with the mutton.

Fiona is downcast and dispirited by the passing events—the last confrontation with Steward among them. It had been her usual practice to check on Steward each evening. Most nights, the knocking on his door went unanswered or she would hear sounds of sobbing and lamenting. One night in particular, much to her surprise, the door swung open with the lift of the door latch, and Steward appeared bathed and dressed for an evening on the town.

"Well, if it isn't Fiona, my lovely wife. Did you come to practice your wiles upon me, my love? Get my blood finally fired?" He asks in a voice that was barely audible, but yet vindictive.

Fiona advances. He waves her off with a swing of his arm in the direction behind her. "Be gone. Go back to your banshees. Look at you! First, go to the reflecting pool and see the image you portray there. You are a sight... and getting quite plump, I might add. Your breasts are full, straining against silk, and leaking colostrums, staining your blouse."

Fiona is trice fustigated by Steward's gritty blows. His vile tirade slaps across her face, leaving a vivid trace of red.

"Why did I ever think you the most beautiful of women... or that you could ever replace another—the only true love in my life?" His voice, like ice, sends bitter chills to her heart.

She covers her face, weeping.

Unbearable Unhappiness.

It was the worst of times. Weeks... days... minutes, moments pass slowly. Young hearts lay heavy with time, trouble, and turmoil. Their childish and unseemly wrangling lead to strained and severed relations... unsalvageable. Both are fully aware that the magic is gone, had passed them by.

Love had come full circle. No time left for talk and tears.

At one of their daily meals, Fiona makes every effort at conversation with Steward, but, as in the past, all proves fruitless. She sits in silence as he sulks through mid-supper.

Once again she confronts him as he is leaving the table: "You cannot be going into town again! I will not allow it!"

She grabs at his coat as he prepares to leave, in an effort to hold him back. Steward spits, "You bitch! There is nothing for me here. I despise you, woman! Why did I ever think…" He stops mid-sentence. There is stinging silence as these words settle in the dark dusty corners of the room.

"Who are you to give commands to me?" Steward demands.

He grabs her and slaps her hard across the face with the back of his hand. Storming out of the room, he quickly makes his way toward the front gateway, oblivious to her cries.

This firm blow causes Fiona to stumble back and fall over the stone pillar at the top of the stairway. She lands face first and stomach second into the gravel walk a few feet below.

Steward, still luminous with fury, shouts back. "Do not try to stop me from leaving, now… or ever again. I will visit… yea, bed… whom I choose, whenever I choose… and I will do what I will with them! I told you once… never interfere."

Fiona sits up angrily… bewildered. She lightly touches her bruised face… and screams out his name through the tears that are welling up in her throat, "Steward!"

Fiona fought deep despair. Hopelessness. Humiliation. As she tries to straighten up, an alarming, dreadful thought boils up from her insides: *Over! Our love is truly over.*

"I have been such a fool," she tells herself. "No matter what I have tried to do to save our marriage, you have cursed my every attempt."

Moments of realization bring her pride to an alarming force as she contemplates her future.

"Well then, Steward, you have made a bad choice leaving me! Two can play this game. If it is a dueling match you want, then be on guard. I will defend myself against your thrust. Courtesy of combat be damned. For you, my dear Steward, the game could be deadly... You may have finally met your match!"

The shadows of evening grew longer and a chill wind began to blow... clearing away the fallen leaves from the stone steps of the bold fortress... and all remnants of obsequious innocence... as well.

CHAPTER FOUR

A Deadly Game.

Filled with absolute angst, her mind spinning, twirling with worry, Fiona reaches out to her friend Una for help once again. She must procure a herbal medicine to settle the queasiness in her stomach, and attend to the bruises on her body, now, immediately. She is extremely concerned about the bleeding she is experiencing since her fall down the stairs, or was it a push? Sometimes the blood comes in droplets; other times, the bleeding is heavier, staining her linen undergarments and her petticoats.

Saving her baby is uppermost in her mind; she is fearful that the baby will be damaged. The child has started to stir within her now, this loving seed of what once was bliss… not the demon seed that Steward alluded to. But growing within her also is her feeling of contempt for her husband, now an execrable stranger to her.

Fiona relates her deep, dark fears to Una. The witch warns her to be ever vigil: "You cannot see the forest for the trees. You must prevent him from putting you in harms way or hurting you again. He threatens the baby you carry. You must talk to the sweet child within you. Tell her each day she is loved, loved with only the heart a mother would know."

Una places an apothecary jar in Fiona's hands and comforts her with her words: "Take this lavender and may oil. When you put the oil on your stomach, rub it in three round circles each time... The oil will give you strength of body. Remember, you are to lovingly caress the child in thought and deed. You must sing blessings to her, as well. She needs to know she is safe... Let the child feel your love and she will have the desire to sleep contentedly inside you."

Una now has Fiona rest on a pallet in the dark light of the camp. An array of scented candles is lit. Una chants in an ancient Gaelic tongue: "Cosaint n ndeithe do Fiona. (May the gods protect you, Fiona)."

A golden and blue column of smoke rises from the cooling cinders smoldering in the fireplace as Una speaks. "You do not see with both your eyes. You do not see the two faces of Stewart. It is time to think clearly with your mind, not with your heart."

Warmly taking Fiona's hand in hers, she traces the lines of the softness of Fiona's right hand, the lifeline, the heart line, the head line, mapped within her palm. Running her fingers slowly along the line of fate in the center of Fiona's hands, Una begins to sway her head back and forth, eyes closed, as if in a trance.

She finally speaks, "Fiona, your life as it is now is not good for you. We must rid your life of evil... for evil is powerfully entwined and tangled around the roots of your problem. Be strong. Put your heart's travailing behind you. Be wise like the owl of the woods. Listen. Learn to resolve and reason judiciously."

"Come," Una continues, "Let us throw the stones of fate for reassurance. I will cast your stones to the four winds, north, south, east, and west, and examine the path before you."

Una throws the 24 thumb-sized Rune stones. Like magic, they land face down on the dirt floor. Although it has been three centuries since the invading Viking introduced rune stones to the highlands, gypsy fortunetellers, mystics, and white witches continue the practice of "throwing stones" to predict the future, heal the sick, and banish evil.

"Pick but one stone," she suggests to Fiona.

Fiona leans forward and chooses, with trepidation, one stone from the 24. The selected stone has a rough looking cross etched on it.

"Reflect on what the stone you now hold means to you," says Una.

After a moment of meditation, perhaps two, Fiona said, "I believe it says that I am at the crossroads between good and evil."

"You have spoken wisely," advises Una, giving an assuring nod of concurrence. Yet, deep in her heart, Una knows full well that the sign of the cross indicates a path filled with sorrow.

"It is time to make a decision about your life."

Fiona decides, "I must protect my unborn baby at all costs. Tell me what I have to do. Instruct me if you will, my friend."

"Yes," say Una, nodding in agreement. "You have chosen the wiser of two fates. You must now rid yourself of the present danger in your life, and allow the seed within you to grow and flourish. I will prepare a special potion for you that will expel the bad so only goodness will prevail. Is this your wish?"

Receiving agreement from Fiona, Una proceeds to make a concoction of Monkshood from the

Ranuncalaceae plant found growing in the dark, damp woodlands. She grinds together the roots, seeds and preflowering leaves of the toxic Monkshood.

"This mixture will be purple in color, like the flower of the plant. Add but a few drops to Steward's daily wine. He will be none the wiser until it is too late... telling us the monkshood has done its damage."

Fiona felt panic surge. Her face turns white and pale with fear. "Is that my only recourse?" she asks anxiously.

"The gods have spoken," Una declares. "Remember, evil begets evil. Evil comes from he who evil thinks. Steward has done many harmful and sinful deeds in his life of which you shall soon learn. Until this present time, you have been unknowingly blinded by love. In the absence of light, darkness waits... and evil prevails."

The Marketplace.

The monotonous mood of the fort was wearisome. Steward, his manners as vile as anyone could imagine, orders Fiona to travel upland to the Castle Baine market to buy his much needed wine-- his life saving elixir--and food to stock the larder kitchen. "Take that foolish handmaiden with you! Leave the scullery maid behind as I quite fancy her," he proclaims on a justificatory note.

Ah, a chance to be reprieved for a day, thought Fiona with a sigh of relief. *I long to breathe the sweet air of the country side—the highlands.*

Fiona quite looks forward to traveling the road to the nearby marketplace. She will be able to talk with her friends and hear the news from the local merchants and artisans. A return to the gossip and folderol of her childhood days at Lockmoor and her many trips to the fair. She pleasantly recalls strolling through Merchant's Row, having her nostrils quiver with delight, challenged by the enticing aromas of the food booths, and the enticing scents of spices, herbs, and perfumes emanating from many of the stalls along the thoroughfare.

She enjoys the sights of the colorful tents and listening to the cacophony of sounds of the merchants hawking their wares, and minstrels singing their original ballads—which they will gladly sell you at a so-called "fair" price.

The bards are able to put the crowd in a gleeful mood. Every fair had one bard, two, perhaps even three. Themes of their tall tales were often on a grand scale... well-known legends of giants and the strength of super men, not to mention, strange tales of the supernatural. They amuse young and old alike, weaving spells to delight. They captivate the audience, entertaining for hours with stories of mystical water beasts, seal women, witches and shamans, and tales of river gods and monsters.

Add to this the thrill of listening to the juicy backstairs gossip. Fiona looks forward to hearing, once again, the spirited music of the fiddlers, fine and talented, and the pied piper, who will pull out his pipe and play you a tune, ever entertaining the lively and rambunctious crowd. It is a mixed conglomerate of rich and not so rich customers, from lords and ladies to beggars and thieves.

Fiona makes plans to starts out at dawn in order to complete her buying and be out of the market place before the uproarious late night "goings on" begin-- carousing, whoring, and gambling-- for she is well aware that many customers seek a full day of entertainment, from sunup 'til sun down, as they are a hardy, daring, and adventurous breed, these highlanders, bent on having their full fill of fun and games, desirous of turning a trick or two.

To keep herself safe from harm, Fiona chooses to travel with her handmaiden and Emil, captain of the guards at Lockmoor. He will be held responsible for driving the horse drawn carriage, keeping a watchful eye on things, and bringing her home "all in one piece" with the valued supplies.

Heaven forbid that something happens to the wine!

In addition to the purchase of jugs of alcohol, Fiona buys bread, salt, dried fish, spices, and pickled meat flavored with vinegar. A wise customer, she knows well how to barter, bicker, and trade with the merchants. In for the penny—out for the pound!

As she readies to leave the market, Fiona's attention is drawn to the tinkling sounds of bells. Her eyes search for the source of the quaint jingling. A beggar is seated at the corner of one of the stalls; she notices his hand on the cord of the bells attached to the stall for decoration. She inquisitively moves closer. He is ringing the bells softly, in a light and gentle way, emotionally susceptive to the senses. The hood of his ragged cloak partially hides his face. Unexpectedly, **the beggar motions to her to come forward. His index finger moves with a "come hither" motion.**

Fiona, intrigued, steps closer, slowly, in apprehension. Nearing him, the beggar holds his tin cup high in the air.

"For me? This is for me?" Fiona queries.

She peers inside the rusty orange cup and spies a shiny object resting at the bottom. The beggar makes a motion for her to take it, literally shoving the old cup into her face. She stands there mystified and quite confused. Gingerly picking the coin out of the cup, she slowly turns to hold the coin up to the sunlight to get the best view.

"Oh my! How beautiful," exclaims Fiona with surprise as she scrutinizes the golden object.

On this striking coin, she spies the bust of a Roman emperor with a laurel wreath in his hair. Fiona soon realizes that she has seen this marvelous coin before, but where? She tugs at her brain for a revelation.

Turning to ask the beggar about the coin, she notes that the raggedy old man has slipped from sight. Only the empty rusty orange cup is sitting on the spot where the beggar had once been. Quickly and silently she stashes the coin away, hiding the golden treasure inside her cloak, then rushes to catch up with Emil, who is hurriedly placing the newly purchased supplies into their small wooden carriage.

Emil is in a dark mood. The handsome Captain has had his fill of fire-eaters, and gypsies reading Torah cards. He is tyrannized by time, with its pressures of expectation. Has the urgency to go! Twilight, as the sunlight scatters, is fast approaching. A snap of the whip makes the carriage bolt forward, and the cadence of hoof beats increases as they head for home, over the firm earth of the roadway.

The Golden Coin.

Later that evening, she retrieves the coin from its hiding place. *I must tell no one of this day... of this coin,* thought Fiona.

Yes! She had seen this bright gold coin once before... in her past. Edmud, Steward's brother had shown the coin to her on one of the moon struck evenings before the wedding at Castle Baine... her most beautiful wedding.

She recalls Edmud explaining that he had bartered for the gold piece on one of his trips to the continent, just across the channel. He said that the coin was of the bust of the emperor Augustalis and was one of the most beautiful and most valuable coins in the western world... worth millions! Edmud had told her of his plan to give the coin to his mother, Lady Kyla, sometime after Steward and Fiona's wedding. He felt the coin reminded him of his mother's treasured golden beauty.

"But how am I able to hold this coin in my hands now?" She pondered the possibilities.

"I must look into this matter... but for now I will hide this golden keepsake in a safe place. I must savor the coin for my beautiful golden child who is soon to be."

Revisiting the Market.

The following fortnight, Fiona decides she will return to the marketplace, putting her troublesome thoughts to rest. She tells Steward that there is a need to buy bread, cheese pies, pickled chicken, and various spices, and other cooking supplies. At first he grumbles at the thought, but soon agrees to her market trip as he is again in great need of ale and wine. He must have sufficient drink stored in the buttery for his daily consumption or, otherwise, his furious temper will erupt in violence… without notice… without regard for anyone he strikes.

"More wine! Is this an omen?"

Fiona happily obliges Steward's new request to return once again to the market as she, herself, is quite drawn to finding the old ragged beggar who had given her the valuable golden coin and solve its riddle.

As always, the noisy marketplace gives Fiona enjoyment. Conversing with her friends, listening to the high spirits of the music and the crowds, the piercing sounds of the bagpipes make her smile. The sound of her own laughter actually startles her for she realizes she has not laughed for quite some time.

Then, almost out of coincidence, she spies the beggar she is searching for. He is seated, right there, by a food stall that is gaily decorated with lively chiming bells. As before, his dark cloak covers half his face. Again he encourages her to come forward with a gaunt finger motion. Her heart starts beating rapidly, leaping like a bouncing ball being thrown by a juggler. She furtively follows him to the side of the food stall.

The stranger speaks. "Don't let me frighten you, but I know you."

Having said that, the stranger pushes back his hood and Fiona sees his face. A clump of wild hair, shockingly white, like the belly of an albatross, sticks boldly out from the top of his head. His face is a ghastly patchwork of red and white burned tissue. His lips are frozen upward in a horrible rictus of a smile.

"I am Edmud."

Fiona is mesmerized by the horror of the distorted sight before her. It takes a moment for her to internalize what the beggar is saying.

"Edmud? Edmud?"

Her face turns ashen, her eyes flash with fear. Stepping back quite afraid, her hand covers her mouth in an effort to silence her sigh of horror.

"Edmud. Alive?" she mouths in disbelief. She draws her cloak tightly around her trying to ward off the chills attacking her spine.

"Yes," declares Edmud, his gaze hawk-like and impervious. "I have come here to warn you. Steward, your loving groom, did this to me... to my face... the night of the fire. I have evidence that he sent his men to be rid of me."

"What are you saying? Why would Steward commit such a dreadful act? Such an atrocity?" asks Fiona, dismay pooling around her, drowning her. She covers her ears in a vain attempt to block out the murderous accusations she is hearing.

Edmud, like a snake, hissed his reply. "He was embittered when Mother turned to me for guidance and love. He is consumed with hate and anger by the fact that he no longer was her number one son."

Fiona was incredulous. "You lie. This cannot be true. How do I know you are telling the truth… You are despicable!"

"I was instructed to give you the golden florin by the ghost of my mother who appears to me each and every night in my dreams. She tells me you would know the coin and know without the smallest doubt that my story is true. Steward is an evildoer. I shiver at the thought of Kyla's screams of pain. He must pay for his sinful murdering," snarls Edmud in all his ugliness. His grotesquely curled smirk is caught in the sun's unforgiving light.

He pleads with one last caveat: "You are not safe with him. Get out now. Escape."

"Help me to understand. I, too, have felt Steward's hateful wrath. There has to be a way to obliterate the evil that surrounds your family… and all who have dared to enter Castle Baine, as well."

"I will escape this curse of evil," Fiona says with determination. Her golden eyes darken in both fear and uncertainty. Mostly fear!

CHAPTER FIVE

The Concoction.

Arriving home to Lockmoor, more convinced now than ever that Steward's life source is a baneful entity that must be eliminated, Fiona willingly mixes together the newly bought wine with the toxic concoction of Monkshood given her by Una.

How quickly love turns into hate.

Ah... a few drops of the grape colored mixture will easily go unnoticed in the wine, as the likeness of the colors of the wine and the poison... are identical!

Drink up dear husband. And let the gods' will be done.

This being said, Fiona's long awaited time begins.

Sexual Proclivities.

As is his habit, Steward sits in silence during each midday meal. He drinks heavily, two or more glasses of wine with the food, and rises promptly to leave for town and his rendezvous with the young woman who has become his favorite harlot, Caty.

In the arms of Caty, Steward can be as immoral as he wishes. Often times he eagerly chooses to participate in the act of sexual fulfillment for hours; his virility seemingly endless and timeless.

Caty learned, early on, that Steward liked to shackle her to the bedposts with leather ropes; she also quickly learns what it feels like to be drawn and quartered like a heifer going to slaughter. Steward is in constant need of hearing his name whispered in passion… or screamed from the rooftop, as well. His sexual demands would surely be found degrading to other women, but Caty is in dire need of the money that is paid to her to do "unthinkable" acts… performed in the name of love. She has mastered her trade well and believes that in order to make a male customer content, she should satisfy his every whim.

His wish is my command.

One evening, Steward bound Caty's hands in shackles and threatened to whip her into submission, but Caty was wise to his threats.

"He has the desires of an sinful man, but he would never harm me," or so she thought.

He also has an air of indifference toward her; often, he would abruptly leave the wench's hot bed, preferring the cold wine room downstairs, to continue drinking and gambling late into the night with the other male patrons at the tavern, so often drunk he has to call for his guard, Emil, to help him mount his horse, and guide him safely home in the night's moonlight, as the rough roads and byways held many unsafe trappings: robbers, beggars, and thieves.

Carousing Continues.

As time passes, Fiona must endure Steward's late night carousing and early morning homecomings, each one becoming more noisy, rough, and raucous. When he arises for the midday meal the next day, Steward, still full of drunken dreams and wine, is sour faced and silent. Few words pass between this husband and wife!

Ultimately, Fiona remains stoic in her plans to help rid the world of this satanic man who glances at her and her swollen belly with hate and loathing burning in his eyes. So… each day… she continues to add a few drops of the purple monkshood mixture to his wine, which he quickly devours like a thirst-starved hound after a rabbit chase.

The thought of eating alone with Steward was not inspiring. He ate sparingly at his meal and picked at his food like a small child. After his many goblets of wine… he would suddenly and roughly push back his chair, stand somewhat unsteadily, demandingly call for his guard, Emil, and these two men, one drunk, one sober, would leave the fortress on horseback and head for raw enjoyment.

As he staggers to the tavern that night, Steward is seemingly angry and disgruntled. He commands his guard, Emil, to wait for him outside the tavern; "Be present when I am ready to leave," he shouts. "Do you hear me!"

Steward does not go immediately to Caty's room because he is not in the mood for any sassing or sexual encounters with his playmate. Instead, he sits at the gambling table, ordering wine after wine for himself and his fellow gamblers. Suddenly, Steward's head starts to pulsate violently as if being pounded with a cloch (stone). There is a burst of light. The penetrating sharp pains last only momentarily.

He stumbles like a crippled blind man to the back of the tavern where he can watch the wild cock fighting games, but once again is struck with another quick sharp pain in the back of his head. The sounds of the bawdy gambling men's shouting and yelling for their favorite rooster to win intensify his pain; with head spinning like a gyroscope, he flees back into the recesses of the tavern.

He tells himself: *Stay calm… all is well…*

His attention turns outwardly from himself toward Caty.

"The bitch has waited long enough for me," he muses; "Let's get on with what I came to do. She had better take my pain away as well."

Steward finds that Caty, growing tired of waiting, is anxious to conclude their love making arrangement of the evening. Steward, not liking to be rebuffed in any way, shape or form, grabs Caty and throws her roughly on the bed of hay.

"Arouse me," he commands.

And she does… quickly.

As he starts to move upon her, a vivid, clear picture of his mother engulfed in flames in the castle tower flashes like a lightening rod across his mind. Steward closes his eyes tightly to shut out the horrid scene. He cries out drunken, slurred words into the night—frightening words. His arms and legs contort as if in a wild spasm; white foam gushes and drips from the corners of his mouth. His head is now thrown back in agony; he looks like a lone wolf baying at the yellow moon. He twists… he turns… and almost immediately, falls heavily upon his mistress of the evening.

Caty panics! Uncontrollable terror streaks across the woman's face. Pinned beneath his dead weight, she screams for help. Her sharp piercing shrieks of fright bring other patrons quickly to her aid. Men pull Steward off of Caty to free her, but she is not free for long. Within minutes, she stands accused of killing Steward in the heat of passion.

Caty is roughly dragged to the main floor of the smelly, noisy tavern. The question of what to do with her until there can be a trial is quickly resolved by the male clientele of the tavern. The drinking and drunken patrons immediately decide to remove her to the town square where she will be thrown into the Idiot Cage for the night.

The Cage, a large wooden like crate, with bars at the sides and top, is used to imprison the idiots of the town and lawbreakers alike… and so… if it is good enough for them, it is good enough for a prostitute!

The slotted openings of the cage allow the public to express their disdain for any of the lunatics or criminals housed within. Actually, Caty's accusers can poke, prod, or whip her with sticks or stones, or any weapon of choice, if they so desired, and some might even choose to urinate on her… perhaps torture her, in any form they saw fit. So it is that Caty must try to survive the Idiot Cage while awaiting her trial by the local barbarian court and jury… But wagers are already being made about the outcome of the trial.

The die is cast. A woman of the highlands is seldom found innocent of any crime, and in this case, to be exact, murder.

Messenger of Death.

Fiona is awakened by the sound of pounding hoof beats, a horse's fast approach. The rider halts at the tall doors of Lockmoor, grabs one of the high, round, iron knockers, and pounds on the gate, sending thunderous resounding echoes throughout the fortress. The din is loud enough to wake the deceased… or, the entire household from dead sleep, for that matter. Guards come running toward the entrance and open the gate for Emil, Steward's trusted guard.

There is an earsplitting cry, "News! Come quick!"

From the frantic tone in Emil's voice, Fiona knows that something is wrong, terribly wrong.

Emil shouts on. "The master is dead, the master is dead… murdered at the tavern… by a whore!"

Fiona, covering her ears, tries to block out the news she is hearing. "Steward is dead?" she asked. Tone incredulous. Her question keeps twirling through her mind. Confusion reigns.

Emil responds, "Yes, murdered… murdered in the act of making love!"

His deadly answer sends a sharp pain through her body and pierces her heart. There is a sudden, forceful movement in her stomach and she quickly grabs her body to hug her unborn child.

"Can this be?" "No! Not yet!" she cries out, and simply sits down onto the stone steps.

Hugging her wide girthed body, she whispers to her child-to-be in a voice filled with anguish, "Peace little one, the gods will take care of us."

Justice is Served.

In Caty's favor, most of the people in the town had accept her in the past, and the local prostitutes, as well, as these promiscuous women were believed to serve a vital role: sexual trainer for the younger men and reliever of the lasciviousness of the older men. The prostitutes also kept all men away from masturbation and sodomy... or so it was alleged.

But at today's unruly trial, Caty is in disfavor. According to Mosaic Law, the villagers are in retaliation of an "eye for an eye" and a "tooth for a tooth" mood, more than ready and willing to punish Caty, the trollop. These barbarians could taste the sweet blood of revenge for the death of one of their rich landowners, a free spending nobleman at that. No harlot should get away with murder to any degree, especially murder during the passionate and wild act of debauchery.

All is lost.

Caty Defends Herself.

Caty takes the stand on a makeshift riser next to the bar. After her night in the Idiot Cage, she indeed looks like a lost soul. Her clothes are dirty and disheveled; her once long and silky red hair lies matted in a nest above her shoulders. In spite of her troubled appearance, she curtsies quite eloquently to the crowd.

"My name is Caty. I only prostitute myself to keep my family alive and fed. Since I was twelve, I have been used. Sheep farmers quite enjoyed bending me over stonewalls and entering me at their will. They would throw a few coins on the ground. I would gravel after them."

She tries to speak on, but the crowd jeers. A voice calls out, "The wench is wasting time! Make her tell us how she killed Lord Steward!"

"Let me show you your Lord Steward!" With that, Caty tears her blouse apart with both hands to expose voluptuous white breasts, nipples, round and pink. As she points to a purple discolored area on both breasts, they jiggle. She says, "This is where Steward bit me... as most of my patrons are toothless, they would never be found guilty."

"Put your clothes on girl"—a shout declares. "I have at least three more girls, bigger and better than you, waiting for me upstairs!" Laughter erupts.

"Enough! Hear her out!" someone declares.

Caty tries to defend herself again. She fumbles, and switches her approach to tell of last evening's events. She proclaims adamantly that Steward called out, "Mother, forgive me!" just before he died.

In a panicked voice, Caty continues her story. She tries in vain to explain that Steward was frothing from the mouth and nose; his black tongue protruding, like the devil himself, trying to flee his very innards. "Something was horribly wrong... I know Steward was poisoned. The bad wine he drank in this very tavern caused his wicked death. I am innocent," she screams, pleading to the court. Her request finds unhearing ears.

The courtroom was, after all, a tavern. No one hears her whimpers of innocence over the clatter and chatter of the local peasantry. And no one gives a damn, except for Fiona, who sits alone in a front row seat in this make shift courtroom… a room that reeks of beer, body odor, and mayhem stew.

The only other person who heard Caty repeat the dead man's last words, "Forgive me Mother!" was Edmud, who chooses this precise moment to stand and address the disorderly crowd.

Edmud Accuses.

Edmud's words cut through the din like ice. "Silence one and all," he shouts. "I must be heard."

His voice resounds chillingly across the room and silence decends on the unruly onlookers. "'Tis I. Steward's brother, Edmud, from Castle Baine, upriver on the Knell."

These words startle the crowd. All glance in the direction of the man dressed in the black hooded cape. Pushing back his hood ever so slowly, Edmud reveals his hideously scared face and patch of white hair.

The throng pushes forward to get a look at the man; they gasps in horror upon seeing Edmud's grotesquely burned face. Complete quiet enters the room for a moment. All see and believe that this man is truly Edmud of Castle Baine… therefore his words are true. Group think mentality.

"If anyone is guilty here, it is Fiona, Steward's wife and mother of his unborn child."

Edmud points and shakes an accusing finger at Fiona. "She is bewitched. She married my brother and planned to steal Castle Baine from him… from me.

She refused to let Steward occupy her warm bed. She forced him into the cold bed of this slut. He would not be dead by the hands of this cheap whore if Fiona had carried out her wifely duties to her husband. Steward disowned her as a wife. I say she is the guilty one."

Fiona sat there a minute, paralyzed by the deadly accusation spilling from Edmud's mouth. Frozen in disbelief, she shakes her head, "No! No!"

She stands slowly, exposing her ripening pregnant body. "I did love my husband," she says, softly, *once.* "I am not the evil one in this room."

Once again, a hush falls over the crowd, momentarily stunned by the words forced upon them. But their attention quickly reverts back to the prostitute and seeking revenge. A talion well taken.

"Caty is the evil one," someone yells from the unruly audience.

Yet another initiates the cry, "Guilty!"

His sole voice is immediately joined by those of others; mob mentality has returned full force.

"Guilty! Guilty! Guilty!" the wild crowd yells, their voices boisterous… out of control.

Hysterical fear rises in Caty's throat. She cries out, "I did nothing!" But all her attempts to plead innocent are drowned out in one deafening uproar.

The rough and rowdy crowd pushes forward defiantly and demands that Caty, the murdering wench, be sentenced to death. Hanged by the neck from the gallows.

The angel of death smiles.

CHAPTER SIX

Final Trip Home to Lockmoor.

Time is of the essence. The darkest day of the year has dawned. Because Steward's untimely demise occurred during this hollowed time of the lunar eclipse, his body must be lowered into the ground before the moon completely blocks the sun... and the laws of the land, like binding customs, need to be abided and enforced. All noblemen must be buried before the sun rises on the next morn. And Steward was once a nobleman—lord of the manor, a nobleman, yes— but his recent actions showed that he was not a noble man.

As her servants ready the carriage to take Steward's body home to Lockmoor, Fiona quietly waits. For the first time, she is filled with overbearing grief and her sobs violently shake her body. *What have I done?*

Then, Fiona hears the words, "What's done is done, Biodh se amhlaidh," and she is strongly embraced by the arms of Una, who strays from the shadows.

"Come home good friend and leave this gruesome task for Noah."

Noah quickly approaches and directs the servants to transfer the lifeless body from the wooden pallet to the carriage, now lined with straw and orange bergamot. Steward's last journey home.

First, oil of jasper and hawthorn are applied to the body, thus making it welcome to the gods. The men have wound a woolen shroud of black around the corpse, tying knots at the head and feet... making him look ominous... telling of evil to come... but still very dead.

"Will Don, the pagan goddess of the Sidhe, Ruler over the land of death, communicate with Steward? Can she stop the evil this man might send to Fiona and the baby?" questioned Noah, as he viewed this dark and foreboding scene.

Internment in the Meadow.

The sun burned through in patches, illuminating fragments of landscape, suspending them in the void until the fog blotted them out again. At that moment, the mist parted like a huge curtain to display the panorama of the solemn burial scene, the freshly dug gravesite... small purple quilts of heather... the cold shadows of tall restless trees long across the meadow... somberness... death.

The body was brought home to the meadow that lay distant from the steep side of the fortress, Lockmoor. A grave's opening is dug, shallow and controlled, so that it faces the east, as it is believed that, one day, at sunrise, the dead will have to face their gods' blessing or curse for all eternity. Mounds of dirt around the grave are covered with freshly cut branches of dark green hemlock and fern. Steward's body has been brought to its final resting place! The dim gloom of this day is oppressive.

The perfunctory burial, beneath the immense and shading oak tree, was attended by Noah, Una,

Fiona, Emil, and several of the trusted servants, who had gathered together in a circular fashion around the ground's opening as Steward's shrouded corpse is lowered, gently, into the shallow inhumation place. It was a sorrowful sight.

Dark rich dirt and loose clay are shoveled onto the cloth-covered body. Fiona shutters, feeling as if the first clods of earth are being shoveled onto her body as well. She senses that a black heavy weight, a stone, has been placed upon her heart. Her love for Steward is slowly choked from within her and she needs to cry out in pain. Fiona's face, ashen, reflects the grayness of grief, and teardrops fall unknowingly from her golden eyes. There is none to console her. Alone, she mourns.

At that precise moment, Una begins her death chant by first asking for the blessings of the gods: "Go raibh beannacht na ndeithe agus ar sinsir ar Steward; may the gods of the fire, water, air, and earth find unity as they bless Steward."

Now, speaking to the gods of nature, the ancient dead, and the Sidhe, Una continues to pray that the power of their spirits flow through her and touch the minds of the living and the dead with healing and goodness. "May all evil be buried here this day. Let earth, sea, and sky lend no fears."

Una finishes her chants of appeasement and pleads for help in warding off any evil demands Steward might have made on the Druid forces. Suddenly, an ill susurrus wind, whispering voices of the dead, blows through the oak trees that stalwartly guard the meadow. A screaming gust of cold air, like the shrill of a bagpipe, follows, mysteriously extinguishing the flickering flames of the thirteen tallow candles surrounding the new grave. Dark gray smoke from the Scotch Broom fire, which had been lit for the very purpose of calming the wind, pirouettes skyward in a mournful display of rage.

Fiona's face turns ashen. *Is this an omen from the gods?* She clutches her heart in fright. *"Can the gods ever be appeased?"*

Noah feels the gods will listen to their pleas and be satisfied with what they have heard here today, but he must make sure on his own. He contemplates placing a huge gallan (standing stone) atop the grave site, one that can not be easily moved, so large in fact, that an evil spirit would think twice before leaving his safe and secure home inside Steward's hollow heart before tackling such a task.

"Yes, the gods can stop Steward's evil... but they need a little help from me. A giant stone will be placed upon this grave, this very day," Noah avows.

Remembering.

Fiona is quite shattered in both mind and will by all the happenings of this darkest day. Feeling quite lost, and alone. It is not easy to bury a husband... One that loved you, and then, quite suddenly, decided not to love you. "Despoused" in such a sudden manner. *I never felt so sad in my life.*

Despondency overcoming her, Fiona seeks asylum inside the fortress. She immediately cuddles up within the large oaken rocker next to a blazing fire in the hearth, trying to thaw her chilling thoughts. As she rocks back and forth, to and fro, in the chair... the chair Steward had brought as a wedding gift, a token of love and admiration, to her, his wedded wife, to be presented the morning after the consummation of their marriage. This "morning gift," or thank-offering, was in compensation for the loss of her virginity... on being a bride chaste and pure.

Thoughts of love... those few happy days together... flooded her mind. *I quite wonder if I ever loved this man.* Her musings moved on to those of her first true love... Tears spill over her ashen face and she tried, unsuccessfully, to spike them away. She wept, alone, unhappy.

Una comes to her side and tries to comfort her, knowing that Fiona's feelings of loss are not healthy for the child.

"What have I done wrong, Una, everyone is turning against me. I am quite afraid."

Evil is as Evil Does.

Una's words are marked with alarm. "The tide will turn in your favor, but I fear we have more work to do," she warns.

The two women talk of the vile accusations that Edmud had made at yesterday's murder trial, and more poignantly, how he had betrayed Fiona under the ploy of friendship by giving her the golden coin in good faith.

Fiona's voice shows anguish. "I fear Edmud. He is more evil than Steward. Castle Baine is rightfully mine!"

It is determined that the only way Fiona's fears can be extinguished is by facing them straight on.

"If you are afraid of his curse, you must take action. You must counteract his treat with a treat of your own. Castle Baine rightfully belongs to you and the child, now. You are entitled to it! The castle will be yours when Edmud no longer rules... is incapable of living there. We must make a pact in order that his evil be turned to himself," says Una vehemently.

"Since Edmud casts an evil curse on you and your child, it will now be reflected back towards him, like his looking into a bright reflective mirror, a looking glass," Una proclaims in a confident voice.

"Come Fiona, together we can combat Edmud's evil."

Clasping hands tightly in a sign of the Coventry, the two women stare into the flames of the fire. Una chants three wishes, times three. Fiona follows her lead and repeats the chant: "May the flame of hatred devour him. May his body be infected with his own evilness ten-fold, and the flames of evil burn his mind, weakening his thinking. May the tine choisricthe (sacred fire) show no mercy to his curses and work against him, word for word, deed for deed."

Their voices, reciting in unison, echo through the emptiness of the great hall. Having performed their hexing chant, Una and Fiona throw newly cut rushes onto the hearth's blaze. It causes the fire to burst instantly into bright white startling flames... the hot flames of revenge. The smoldering sparks diminish and dark gray smoke seeps slowly into the room. Fiona drops to her knees in prayer.

"We will survive this day," Una states.

But this day is not yet complete for Fiona and Una.

CHAPTER SEVEN

Home from the Tavern.

Light misty rain is falling that evening as Edmud crosses the soggy moor returning home to his beloved Castle Baine. A vespertine fog has crept over the rolling land partially concealing the castle in inky and gloomy darkness, but he would know his way home even if blind, as he knows this route like he knows the back of his hand. Home—where the heart resides.

This eventful day has proven to be one of great self-satisfaction for Edmud, for he feels that he has accomplished much. His spirit is lifted beyond elation with the knowing that the castle is now his very own; no contenders live! Steward is stone cold dead and buried in the meadow at Lockmoor...

"HA! Good riddance... you evil bastard!" he mutters satirically to himself, *"Castle Baine is now mine!"*

Thoughts of how shrewdly he had played his hand in the "courtroom" today scamper through his mind like prized hunting hounds chasing their prey. He has outfoxed the fox!

"Yes, Steward had a sinister plot to take over this castle for himself, but he was such a fool and he surrounded himself with fools. Did Steward really imagine that he could so dreadfully harm our mother and live to tell about it? Now I have only his simpleton of a wife to contend with... and she doesn't have the brains that the gods gave a wild goose!"

"A pox on you, Fiona! May the devils find you," he pronounces into the mist filled night.

Edmud muses on: You never helped me be rid of your husband... my dear stepbrother... the evildoer... Steward. In the end, it was a prostitute who murdered Steward during their illicit and perverted loving making! But you, Fiona, forced Steward into her welcoming arms.

"Oh, how grand a finish, oh noble brother!" Edmud laughs aloud now, as he cannot control the maniacal glee that engulfs his entire body and soul; it filters into the black chambers of his heart!

Edmud is still chuckling to himself as he crosses the moat surrounding Castle Baine. His horse's cleft hoofs echo a loud cloot, cloot, clooting sounds on the wooden drawbridge leading to the castle's entry. Furious that his access is barred by the twelve-foot iron portcullis, he angrily calls out for the gatekeeper to open the mighty gate. Minutes pass before the guard, struggling with the weighty winch and chains, raises the heavy iron grating. Edmud pushes on the next set of wooden doors. They slowly yawned open, allowing Edmud entrance to the castle.

"Triathanach, mindless peasant," rebukes Edmud.

"But sire, I am alone at my post, I could not see you coming," responds the guard to Edmud, who seems to have momentarily forgotten that the disastrous fire has brought many changes to the defenses of Castle Baine.

Some of the castle's workers have been dismissed and sent away, leaving but a few able-bodied servants to help keep the castle in order and the larder well supplied; only a handful of hale and hardy men now guard the castle against the enemy.

Edmud, himself, has ordered that all the men work at renovating the east tower. These workmen now spend each waking hour rebuilding the tower's gapping black hole, making it livable again. There is the constant tap-tap-tapping of hammers as the masons busy themselves with the challenging task of tearing down the charred blackened wood and reshaping the stone to fill the void boldly eaten away by the hot, fierce, red flames.

As before, Edmud will choose to camp in the Great Hall with its huge log burning fieldstone fireplace, warming his cold and tired feet by the fire, the only source of heat and warmth for the huge, damp castle. A pot of mutton stew bubbles in the pot suspended over the kindling fire within. The pertinent thought he entertains now is giving his wearily aching bones some rest as the day has taken a marked toll on both his body and mind. He will later seek out his bed, to lie under covers of fur, brown and warm. He will drink, and he will try to sleep... to sleep... and to dream. He knows that again tonight he will have those haunting visions of his mother, Kyla. He sleeps... he dreams... in turmoil and turbulence.

As is his vigilant practice now, Edmud makes a cursory inspection of the castle, daily, checking the condition of every richly hand sewn tapestry which had been bought from the continental markets, cargoed up the River Knell on barges, and finally hung gallantly from the high gray stone walls, not only adding sophisticated beauty to the chilly rooms, but keeping out the drafts, as well.

He had brought many of these fine hand stitched tapestries especially for Kyla; she greatly enjoyed the heavy cloths that depicted beasts—real creatures, as well as mythical monsters—in their elaborate designs. He would thrill to the bone hearing her cries of delight with each new purchase he brought back from the world market. Yes, he was far and beyond a shrewder trader and businessman than most... and a more dedicated and loving son than Steward.

Daily Routine.

Taking full account of what is his now that Steward is dead becomes his uncontrollable obsession. He checks on every livestock animal, counting every horse in the stable, and every pig, chicken, and sheep in the field. He counts every leaded and golden goblet and every pewter plate in the hand-carved wooden cupboard in the keep. He must be completely assured that everything of value that had belonged to his Kyla now belongs to him. Every item must be duly accounted for and properly placed.

"Let no item or animal belonging to Castle Baine be lost or stolen by the untrustworthy, treacherous servants, or mendacious peasants working the field," he steadfastly reminds himself. *"Trust no one."*

He evaluates the tower's new construction work, day after day, week after week. He scrutinizes the precision of every stone set in mortar in the new tower. He walks the wooden planks to check their proper placement. The reconstruction is near completion, but Edmud finds the need to make absolutely certain that the tower is resurrected in the same likeness as it was then … when Kyla was alive and loving.

In the early evenings, the air is full of soft fine mist that dithers between fog and rain and covers the castle grounds with flat drops of water. After his perfunctory inspection of the castle, Edmud, habitually, sits in the chilling Highland wind that sweeps through the courtyard. He clutches his fur-lined cape tightly to his neck in an effort to ward off the chill and the dispirited feelings that are his body's constant companions of late.

He pours himself a drink of golden brew. Throwing his ermine lined hood over his charred grotesque face, he crouches, hunched and hidden, recoiled in a state of near madness, and sips the cold ale. The more ale he imbibes, the more he laments about the pleasantries of his youth… he pushes his black depression to the dark recesses of his mind… and this is good. His wanted escape from reality realized.

Thoughts of his mother constantly torment his psyche as he tries to relive the early years of Castle Baine but his memory wanders. He is repeatedly struck by relentless bouts of abject gloom and anguish… his life is unbearable now… gone is his once perfect life… his good life.

Some one has to be the blame for all the angst and desperation he is feeling, but who?

Remembering the Good Times... and Bad.

Kyla became his stepmother many years earlier when his father, a widower banker and merchant, then in his fifty-fifth year, married her. This rich and powerful older Baron brought treasure chests of gold and silver to Castle Baine, and young Edmud, his only son, as part of the marriage arrangement set forth by royal contract.

As a young lad, he remembers that first time he saw the great castle with its red and gold banners, atop the distant east and west towers that rose like stalwart sentinels, blowing and flapping loudly in the wild wind, like large birds attempting to take flight, and the stained glass window of the keep glistening in the sun, sending beams of light to welcome him. For the first time in his young life, he felt that he was going to a new place that would make his life complete. For Edmud, the castle was a magical and mystical sight and he vowed, right then and there, that this mighty castle would someday belong to him.

Edmud's life at the castle proved to be middling. He lived, constantly, in fear of his older stepbrother, Kyla's son, Steward, who had threatened him from the first day he set foot on Castle Baine soil. Could it be that Steward could read his mind? Was he aware of Edmud's thoughts of taking over Castle Baine?

Steward was forever reminding Edmud of his place within the hierarchy of castle possessiveness. "This castle is mine and will never belong to you. You are not a true descendant here; true blood does not run through your veins. Never will you wear the coat-of-arms of the Baine family, I will see to that!"

In simple children's games of catch and knicklestones, Steward would whip the hard ball of wound string at Edmud's face as if the boy was a target rather than a catching partner. In Hoodman Blind, when Edmud had his hood reversed and had to catch one of the other players in the game who buffeted him with rolled-up hoods, Steward chose every opportunity to push... and to shove his blind victim, delivering blows with his fist, oft times blackening an eye or loosening a tooth. A hard belting blow often knocked Edmud to the ground. Splat!

"You will rue and live to regret the day you ever set foot on Baine soil, I'll see to that!" repeated Steward with a defiant smirk.

Frustrated and upset, Edmud refused to cry... and refused to "cry wolf."

In contrast to his initial hatred for his stepbrother, Edmud loved his new mother Kyla. The boy saw Kyla as a golden lady, an angel in disguise, celestial and wise. He found her to be a protective mother; he adored the way she would hug him to her skirts, and brush back his hair from his forehead to calm him anytime he had a fight or squabble with Steward... a frequent occurrence, indeed.

Lady of the Castle.

To his young admiring eyes, Lady Kyla always presented the perfect image. Edmud likes the way the maid has braided Kyla'a long golden hair and hid it under a wimple, a linen band that went under her chin, covered by a white cap of stiffened linen... she was truly a beautiful lady—and wore this beauty so casually.

Sometimes, Kyla, accompanied by her maid, would go down into the outer bailey to stroll in the brilliant sunshine of the walled garden that his father had made especially for her. His new mother loved its exquisite array of flowers, the lilies, marigolds, roses, and gillyflowers, its neatly groomed gravel paths, mulberry trees and climbing vines.

Now and again, Edmud would be allowed to go along with them on their ramble down the garden path. When Kyla held his small hand in hers, he felt loved. She would point out the row of beehives and the newly finished dovecote, a small house with compartments for nesting pigeons. Together they'd laugh as the birds took flight, frightened away by the sound of their voices. Memorable of all, was the sight of the maids, working in the garden, who curtsied low to Lady Kyla as they passed. He thought his heart would burst with pride on seeing his new mother so adored... a proper lady, indeed... to whom he pledged his youthful devotion

On rare times, after the late day meal, Kyla would read to Edmud from her favorite book of poetry. The words of the lively rhyming verses seemed to hold special meaning for her. She would laugh and she would cry. But always she would pull the boy close to her before she sent him off to his room.

Putting her lips close to his ear, she would whisper softly. "You are happy here at Castle Baine, are you not? I need you to tell your father how pleased you are with me as your new mother. You can do that... can you not?"

Of course Edmud would tell his happy little stories to his father as Kayla had asked. He was learning to love her; she had a magic quality that seemed to surround her, an aura of undeniable loveliness. She mesmerized him.

Kyla ably accomplished any task, large or small, with great skill, erudition, and flair. When his father was away attending to his duties in the counting house of the king, and overseeing every royal purchase from the continental markets, Kyla ruled the household.

Kyla was the clever lady of the castle, most knowledgeable about keeping rule in the house and keeping the servants in order. Overseeing the work of the household servants and supervising the small dairy, garden, and kitchen were among her responsibilities. She was fair in her treatment of the servants, provided that each did his allotted share of the work—and did it properly, without skimping by a wink or a whisker—or, until anyone made the serious mistake of crossing her.

She made certain that the needed clothing for the entire family was completed and ready, including the spinning, weaving, and sewing of cloth for each outer and under garment. Being in charge of the keys to the cupboard, the wine cellar, the larder of food, and the keep, where weapons and prize possessions were safely locked away, placed Kyla in a powerful position of control, to be sure.

Noble guests loved her because of the way she would present them with plentiful feasts and fine foods to devour, and place them "above the salt", a seat of honor, at banquets. But the servants hated her because of the way she fed them so little, naught but a bowl of porridge at times.

Servants be damned! thought Kyla.

She never fed the servants the bread plates, called trenchers, at the end of the meal, but rather, she ordered these succulent gravy soaked breads, or any leftovers, for that matter, be fed to the prized, but hungry, hunting dogs which were her only "true" friends in the castle. She especially favored her Irish Wolf hounds, the largest of all dogs, with enormously proportioned bodies. In Celtic legend, such hounds were famed for their ability to pull riders of attacking armies or murdering enemy garrisons down from their saddles with one quick snatch of their massive jaws. Dogs—man's best friend.

Problem with the servants was quickly solved. Kyla would order that offenders be whipped for their complaining or their dishonesty. She trusted no one. Kyla readily kept a sharp eye on the food issued to the cook--so many eels and eggs, so many pounds of rice, so much beef--she would ascertain that all the allotted food, salt, and spices ended up on the family table where it belonged, not hidden in someone's pocket, or the cook would be taken to task in front of the other servants, and punished severely.

She watched the baker closely, too, as bakers were well known for their dishonest tricks. But Kyla did, on rare occasions, reward the honesty of the servants; she never refused to pay them a full day's pay for a very, very, long and full day of hard work.

Family Discipline.

Kyla took control of the obedience of her "two" sons. In training the children to behave chivalrously, Kyla found Steward to be the child in need of strict discipline. For punishment, he was hit or flogged. On one occasion, Kyla took a black leather riding crop to the boy because he had been dishonest; he had the audacity to lie to her. More than once he was harshly reprimanded for stealing precious food from the larder, or letting a prize warhorse out of the stable. He was the incorrigible son.

But Edmud observed a strange phenomenon about Kyla's disciplinary practices. After she whipped Steward for stealing… and unleashed her anger… and calmed down… her harsh mood drastically changed. She would then try to make amends for having punished him too harshly. She would seize the crying boy, lift him onto her lap, push his head to her bosom, stroke his hair softly, and rock him back and forth in a grand effort to silence his sobbing.

Once, after a serious beating, Kyla send Steward to his room. Later in the day, she would go to his sleeping-chamber. Edmud was wise to this because he had become a skilled observer; he noted the jingle jangle of Kyla's keys as she walked down the hallway toward Steward's room. When Edmud peeked into his stepbrother's room, he discovers his "new" mother lying down next to Steward in the fur-blanketed bed, stroking his back, their warm bodies… touching.

Edmud decided that he, too, needed to feel her softness… he wanted her to fuss over him. So he stole apples from the larder, or beat one of the prized hunting dogs in order to be rewarded with tender stroking, or a motherly bedroom visit.

From his first infraction onward, Edmud learned that if he wanted, or needed, Kyla's touch, he could purposely do something naughty... break some rule that would necessitate his submission to a thrashing and being sent to his room. Now he could reap the ultimate benefits... his mother coming to his bedchamber... lying next to him... soothing him with whispered words... giving him her warm and loving attention.

CHAPTER EIGHT

Quarreling Youths.

As Steward and Edmud grew, so did their arguments and loud quarreling. This mandated Kyla's enrolling her sons to chapel school. The boys remained in constant competition with each other. Who could compose the finest written letters, readily read a manuscript, or count to the highest number? In most of their studies and book learning, Edmud succeeded in outperforming Steward at every turn, as it had become blatantly obvious that Edmud had inherited his mathematical prowess from his father.

In his uncontrollable frustration, Steward vowed to avenge his jealousy of Edmud on a level playing field—the field of combat. And Steward did succeed in his campaign. He stood victorious in the mock battles held during practice tournaments for the young knights-in-training. On the first pass with swords and the second pass with lances, the score was usually "evenness" of points between these two ardent competitors. But, by the fourth and final pass of the joust, Steward succeeds in knocking Edmud from his warhorse, to be declared the victor, the goodly knight.

Not only was Steward an excellent horseman, but he was also deft in fighting sword upon sword in dueling competitions: in mock battles, he was quick to knock Edmud off his feet and onto the muddy wet ground. This forced Edmud to beg for mercy, which more than validated Steward's feeling of arrogance and power. He would stride over to where Edmud lay muddied; place his booted foot triumphantly on Edmud's chest, daring him to move... declaring loudly, "To the victor belong the spoils!"

"Edmud, you are scarcely worthy to wear the crest of Castle Baine. And I will see to it that you never do!"

And so, Steward is proven to be the winner at tournament games, games of chance, or games of love. He not only demonstrated that he was the strongest and bravest of the two young knights, but he acquired a charm that ingratiated him to women, wooing the ladies of the day... and the ladies of the night. Steward became a knight in shining armor to many, albeit any, damsel in distress, including his own mother, Lady Kyla. And an icon to himself.

Initially elected to serve and protect the neighboring barons from land skirmishes, a post at which he was, at times, a spectacular success... and, at times, an abject failure... Steward was ordered home to protect Castle Baine, its land and its treasures, from plunder and assault. Victorious youthful jousts and equestrian prowess proved to be a tremendous training ground for Steward. The transition from bully fighter... to bully leader of the garrison of comrade soldiers and men-at-arms stationed within the castle was simple... and elementary!

As luck would have it, Castle Baine's armourer willingly aided Steward in his duties, helping him by checking the stocks of lances, swords and mail. Bowstrings and arrows, especially the short heavy bolts for the crossbows, were kept in good order, and the reddish rust coating was erased from the chain mail by this diligent servant who rolled them in barrels of sand mixed with vinegar until all the rust, caused by exposure to the elements of moist air, magically disappeared. Naturally, Steward took all the credit for how fine and dandy the soldiers-at-arms presented themselves.

In the role of captain of the guards, Steward was quick to win over the respect of his fellow knights, albeit pseudo, even though his actions were, oft times, wild and reckless. If veneration were not granted him, Steward would not hesitate to throw a guard or two into the Castle's dark, dark, dungeon to play with the rambunctious rats… or to order extra practice of skills of lance and sword in the courtyard, to the amusement of all onlookers.

To be on the safe side, the guardsmen found it to their advantage to travel and drink with Steward, and in time, all wisely vowed Steward, their fearless, handsome leader, their allegiance. Steward, contentedly wearing the bright red and gold crest of Castle Baine, found himself in rigid control of bullying leadership. He would strut across the castle's wall-walk and look out across the land—the vast highlands. He was the king of all he surveyed. Loving the power. Feeling like the cock of the walk.

Obsessed with watching others, Steward became an ever-present observer at Castle Baine, a position of empowerment he truly treasured, undeniably. He knew every step his mother took. He scrutinized her every movement about the castle… closely, caringly. He easily kept a close eye on Edmud. He keep track of his stepbrother's absences from the castle… and his returns with gifts and wares from the continent. He knows to whom the gifts are being given. He has spied on the welcoming homecomings, not happy with what he sees.

"Do not try to fool me with your goings and your comings, Edmud. I know your game!" *I am the better player.*

Steward quietly observes the twilight each night as the purple clouds bruise past the moon. It is the twilight of his beloved Highlands. His home. Why does it not bring peace? Inner peace? Has he been too busy with his own thoughts, and so consumed by his hatred of Edmud?

Hatred, it festers and blisters like a boil—on the hind end of mankind. In dire need of lancing. Eradicating all the poisons within.

The twilight is lengthy. The sun hovers on the horizon. Not unlike a tiresome guest on the doorstep— lingering too long… way past it's welcome. Knowing it will be never invited back again.

He listens to the birds above. They soar. Soaring high on the afternoon thermals—scarcely ruffled by the late afternoon wind.

Is all well in the highlands, one wonders? As the highlands offer no fondness—no hope—no love! Are these things important?

Weighed and measured, one brother follows the moon, the other, the stars.

Edmud, Traveling Tradesman.

As Edmud grew older, he followed in his father's footsteps and established himself as a superior tradesman... ever tallying money spent and debts owed, tit for tat. On his first trip, he had accompanied his now ailing father to the great trade routes that were located on the continent, from Italy to Flanders. When he traveled alone, he decided on the world market of Brie and Champagne, France.

Away from Castle Baine, Edmud continued to feel the need for his mother's love and affection as his reward. Such became paramount in his mind. At the world markets, Edmud constantly searched for the perfect gifts to surprise his mother... as he had grown to love to bring her fine presents... and she had grown to love to receive them.

He brought Kyla precious offerings from abroad... spices from the Orient, silver or gold, bolts of fabric, brilliantly colored hand-sewn tapestries to garnish the castle walls, perhaps a valuable oil painting or two from France. To his pleasure, she thanked him fiercely by giving him a long and memorable embrace.

He remembered how Kyla would cry out ebulliently. "Such largesse! Such generous gifts! How lovely... and just for me. You are the most thoughtful and loving son, my dear handsome Edmud."

Remorse.

"But now, since Kyla's death, and the deadly fire in the castle's east tower, my life has changed, forever..." Edmud sobs uncontrollably as he rambles on, tears wetting his severely scared face.

"My hideous face condemns me... prohibits me from leaving this castle, to be a part of the world. I have no gifts to buy or bring. Kyla... dead... out of my sight. I will see her beauty ever again. I only have her spirit in my dreams. So I must go to sleep... to sleep... and to dream. I must visit my sweet Kyla, in my dreams."

Quickly, his mood shifts from morose to vindictive. "Steward is dead now. Yes! But his wife, Fiona, must fear my wrath! Murderers! I blame you both with Kyla's murder."

He cries out into the dark silent night, in rage.

"Fiona! You, too, must pay for having taken love away from me... and so must Steward's unborn child!"

"I vow to right the wrongs done at Castle Baine."

A Reason to Visit Fiona.

In the wee small hours of the morning, yellow illuminating light trips in from the golden moon, high in the sky, orchestrating the eerie shadowy world of the castle. The shiny orb travels from west to east. Edmud, suffering from far too much ale and marked sleeplessness from dreams that did not come, leaves his cold bed, his feet not warmed by the hot coals the servants had placed there. He crawls up the narrow spiral stairs of the west tower, step by step, to his counting house… the room where he has sequestered away his trove of treasures, well hidden under the wooden eves, away from any and all intruders.

He empties a small bag of valuable coins once hidden in a key locked chest; he empties brown leather bags filled with shiny rings, jeweled brooches, priceless silver cups and dishes onto the large table and gazes at his riches—mesmerized by his grand fortune.

Running his knurled and scared hands lovingly through his cherished coins, he begins to parsimoniously count out his money, one… two… three… First, he counts out his many silver coins, biting one or two along the way, checking their density of metal. Then, in dismay, he pauses to reflect about his pile of gold coins… his grand fortune.

"Now, mother, where is that lovely golden coin I brought home for you, the emperor's coin?" Edmud ponders, momentarily paralyzed.

""Gods help me, I remember now," he cries out in a terrified voice, his heart racing, his mouth dry.

I gave that very valuable golden coin to Fiona, like Mother instructed me. And the coin worked like a charm. Through its power, I was able to convince Fiona of my honesty. Such a gullible peasant! Now it is time to get the magic coin back and give it to its true owner.

"That special golden gift will make mother happy again," Edmud declares. "I will retrieve what rightfully belongs to Kyla – the valuable golden coin of Augustalis that matches Kyla's beauty - and return it to its rightful owner.

Finding Fiona and the Golden Coin.

Within a fortnight, Edmud readies himself to set out for Lockmoor to retrieve his gold. The last many months have been unbearable for him for he has been unable to give his esthetical Kyla a gift, a wonderfully desired gift. Now he will have that special opportunity to see her beautiful face smile at him again when the coin is returned to Castle Baine... given to its just owner. When Kyla comes to him in his dream, he will place the golden gift in her hand, and she will hug and caress him, and stroke his hair, as in the past. The thought of being loved again taunts him, sending deep warm tremors throughout his gaunt body... down to the very soul of his haunted heart.

Edmud chooses his horse, haphazardly mounts him, and rides off in the dreary morn in search of Fiona's fortress. The ghostly white curtain of fog parts in front of him. Ill prepared for the trip, he carries no weapons but the small dagger hidden in the waistband of his breeches.

The iron portcullis of the castle is up and opens onto the misty moor that surrounds much of Castle Baine. Edmud's horse strides through the purple heather that crowns the fields with vibrant color, the horse's hoofs sinking, at times, into the soft peat ground. His steed gallops on through the fields—each a slightly different shade of green. But Edmud does not seem to notice, as he is intent on his mission of retaliation.

On horseback for better than an hour, Edmud, feeling weak from lack of food and sustenance, realizes he must stop at the marketplace for something to eat, be it water... be it bread. He knows this area well as he once was a trader at the busy market, and many of the populace, dressed up in their finest clothes, would sally forth to purchases gewgaws--trifling pieces of finery. Baubles! Bangles! Rare gold and silver coins and trinkets of delight.

Throwing his cloak over his head to hide his face, he dismounts, encounters the first food tent, and buys one small trencher of pork stew, smothered in spices and greasy gravy, and to wash it down, one large jug of dark ale. He miserly counts out the cost of two pence from his travel bag to pay for his meager purchases.

Edmud devours the spicy food quickly, dripping and dribbling dark juices down the front of his black cloak. He slugs down his brew in a few large gulps. He speaks to nary a soul in the marketplace, as being at the market only serves as a grim reminder of what his life used to be... one of joy, adventure, trading, and love... before he was touched by the curse of fire and brimstone.

Resuming the last part of his journey toward Lockmoor, Edmud imagines how he will confront Fiona and retrieve his precious coin. His eyes are painfully squinting at the hot sun beating down on his scared face; his stomach is rolling and tossing from the quickly eaten meal... or maybe from the uncooked greasy lamb itself that had been his first food of the last few days.

In spite of his trials and tribulations, persevere he must, as there is a job to be done here, a trick to be played, and a prize possession to be won back from the slow-witted wench Steward had chosen to marry.

Edmud finds his way to the green brambled meadow that lies to the east of the fortress. He had planned to ride up to the high front door, pound the lion-faced knockers, and, when the door was opened, demand his treasure. He would promise that more coins, albeit of lesser value, would follow as a gift for Steward's baby, due within this time of the full moon.

Suddenly, an ax, propelling swiftly through the air, accurately slices though the wide trunk of an oak tree directly in front of him, so startling Edmud's horse with its suddenness that the animal wildly rears up on his haunches, forcing Edmud to loose control of the reins, slide from his saddle, and land firmly on the ground. Splat!

Within seconds, he finds his neck held in a vice; gripped as tight as the teeth of a hunting hound grabbing the throat of his prey. Edmud, his lungs gasping for air and life, desperately tries to uncoil the wench grip of his attacker from around his scrawny throat.

Holding a blade to Edmud's head, the man bellows into his ear. "Intruder, you do not belong here!"

It is the voice of Noah. With massive arms, he hold Edmud as his prisoner, slowly forces him flat onto the ground. Prostrate! Biting the dust.

Noah continues his guttural roar of annoyance. "You trespass where you are not wanted!"

"Help me!" Edmud gasps the only words he can eek out. He speaks in rapid bursts. "I have come to see Fiona. I need to give her a message. I have a vital message for her and her child to be. I bid you tell her to meet with me this very day!" Edmud urgently pleads.

"Aye, and what am I going to do with you in the mean time?" questions Noah sarcastically. I do not trust you here alone in this place while I go in search of Fiona."

Pausing for a moment, Noah is struck with an intriguing idea. "Wait! Wait! I know you will not be alone if I leave you here, alone, when I go to do your bidding. The spirit of your dear dead brother, Steward, guards this meadow now, and his ghost will see to it that you do not flee until I bring Fiona to you. You will be a very foolish man if you move one step. Do not stray a jugfull!" Noah warns persuasively.

With no alternative, Edmud must do as he is told. He waits in dreaded fear, rubbing his crushed throat and body in an effort to ease the pain, as Noah moves out toward the fortress to fetch Fiona.

Noah finds his mistress in the great room of the fortress, sitting quietly in the carved oaken rocker. She is rubbing her swollen body soothingly with her hands. Beside her is a tray of food and drink, left untouched; sudden sharp stomach pains have taken away her need for nourishment. A heavy strangeness has overcome her, as well, for she realizes the baby within has become very still… motionless.

As Noah approaches, Fiona rises very slowly to greet him. Noting his red flushed face, she asks alarmingly, "Noah, what is wrong? Tell me! Please!"

Noah blurts out his story of Edmud being in the meadow this very day, and proudly boasts that he ambushed the man into swift and total submission. He also relays Edmud's request to meet her in the meadow... but in his own mind Noah knows of the danger. *Beware of this enemy who has approached.*

At first, Fiona is jolted by the news of Edmud's presence here, at her fortress, and on her property.

"I made the mistake of trusting him once... I was a fool. I will not make that mistake again," declares Fiona in an upset tone.

"Perhaps, my Lady, this is not a good time to be out in the meadow with Edmud. Your baby is almost ready to arrive. You should not be doing this, you should not be out," says Noah, in a voice full of concern.

"But if you choose to go to Edmud, I will protect you with my life," adds Noah.

Fiona wraps her woolen shawl around her full body in an effort to steel herself for her trip into the lion's den.

"I must do what has to be done. I must face Edmud, and I will be threaten by him no longer," she declares.

Fiona calls for her trusted servant Emil to assist her on the walk to the meadow. "Come, let us depart now while I am free from thoughts of pain."

Moving slowly from the fortress to the meadow, Emil and Noah aid Fiona every step of the way, least she might stumble on the rough clumps of briars and wild crawling vines that cover the terrain.

They find Edmud where Noah said he would be. Still stunned and shaken by the possibility of Steward's attacking ghost, Edmud sits, vigorously guarding himself, for he had nowhere to run... and nowhere to hide. His small dagger, a "Sgian Dubhs," has been drawn from his waistband and held tightly in his bony fist. With this three inch bladed weapon, Edmud is jab, jab, jabbing the circle of air that surrounds him, defending himself against all possible evil intruders who just might have decided to come and pay him a visit, as Noah had warned.

Edmud is more than pleased to see Fiona. He feels safe now, protected from any ghostly attacks. Wasting nary a moment, he discloses his special mission to Fiona.

"I am here to buy back the golden coin I gave you at the marketplace. It is of no value to you, an almost worthless coin... but it is a coin close to my very soul as it reminds me of Kyla... my mother. I will give you other coins of equal value and then some, if only you will return that special coin to me," Edmud pleads.

Alarmed by his request, Fiona is confused and taken back momentarily. "You will pay me equally for the coin?" asks Fiona quizzically, her brows knotting together into a deep frown.

"I can be trusted," assured Edmud, with a disingenuous smile. It was a horrible, frightful smile.

His words send a chill of doubt through Fiona's mind and body as she remembers how she had trusted him before, *with fool-hearted results.*

"This I will do," Fiona decides, "I can plan to bring the coin you seek back to you... soon... and we can make an equitable exchange of coins, as you promise. The exchange must be fair."

At this moment, Fiona knows in her own mind that she will pray to The Vates, the wise gods, who will know if Edmud is speaking the truth... or if he is full of taradiddle. And she will again have Una cast her stones to the wind to explore this new path that lies before her.

Fiona tightens her shawl around her to ward off her bone chilling thoughts and she prudently continues.

"But for now, Noah will lead you to the roadway that will lead you back to Castle Baine. You must leave this meadow immediately, and do not return. You are unwelcome here."

"Done."

Just as Edmud replies, a black shadow from an early evening cloud crosses his face, marking it with a repulsive look of evil.

CHAPTER NINE

The Dark Route Home.

Edmud thankfully sets off along the dusky route home, content to leave the fortress with its strangeness and peril far behind him. He is filled with emotions that range from the sublime to the bizarre; he has a calm feeling of peace for having confronted Fiona about his golden coin; he has superior feelings for having fought off Steward's ghost that guarded the meadow. HA! But his feelings of self pride converge with a frantic and frenzied feeling of pointed regret… his head aches with poignant pings of failure… he had so wanted to have his precious coin, his piece of gold, in his very hands, at this very moment, as a gift for Kyla, as promised… this very night.

Billowing cumulus clouds gather in the early night's sky as Edmud's horse trots on toward Castle Baine. Darkness settles in. Slowly passing the marketplace, the unwelcome din of boisterous voices attack his ears.

"HA! Those rowdy drunkards and sleazy gamblers at the fair will carouse till the wee hours of the morn."

No! He never had any use for such bogart men, cut-throats, with their wild and woolly ways.

"Those fools are as barbarian as Steward had been throughout his useless life… but alas… Steward is dead… it was all for naught. *HA*! More's the pity!"

He feels a sharp jolt—a nudge that throws him off guard. Edmud panics! He curses the night and its looming darkness, and reprimands himself for not bringing a servant along to carry a lantern or a torch to light his way, when, miraculously, out of the dimness, a rising full moon shows its face, a silver beam in the night sky, illuminating his safe return to the castle. Edmud emits a sigh of relief.

Reaching the moor, Edmud praises himself for his ability to arrive home safely. Although his breathing has returned to normal, he is still plagued by an aching gut, rolling and tossing like a ship at sea, sick and sour.

"I need to forget my ills. It is time to celebrate my success of this day... the golden coin of Augustalis will soon be mine again," he muses contentedly.

Clump, clump, clumping across the castle drawbridge, he finds, to his distinct pleasure, the iron gate is up and he rides his horse directly into the courtyard, satisfied that the guards had been aware of his approach and opened the portcullis for him. He is home... and he is happy.

Dismounting slowly, Edmud enters the Great Hall. He realizes his feelings of triumph must be nourished; the best way to do that is with a toast, to himself, the victor of the day. Opening a jug of ale, he quickly splashed the golden liquor into a goblet, raises it high into the air, toasts his praises and good fortune, adamantly, and slugs down the brew with great abandon. The ale is soothing to Edmud's aching body. So he drinks another, and another, as the shadows from his mind take over the room. He has a feeling he is not alone.

Within an hour, he is in a euphoric mood, anxiously looking forward to his sleep, to his dreams, to his visit from Kyla in the night. He apprehensively awaits the moment when he can tell her about the return of the coin of Agustalis, the most valuable coin of the realm.

But before his expected dreamtime bliss, one vital duty lies ahead. He must properly inspect the east tower and evaluate the labors that have been completed in his absence.

"Castle Baine must be washed clean of every last mark of the tower fire, the fatal flame, the apocalypse, that changed his life forever. Every black mark from the past must be obliterated from the present. Every evil sign of that horrific night must be eradicated from all the stone.

The castle must be cleansed, from black to white!

Checking the East Tower.

With no small amount of effort, Edmud pushes himself to his feet. And then he just stood there, swaying like a willow in the night wind. Trying to regain his balance, he staggers, zigzagging across the graveled courtyard. He pulls open the wooden door of the East Tower.

Climbing up the steep and shadowy stairway to the top, one slow confronting step at a time, Edmud reaches the tower at last. He finds, to his contentment, that the work on the top floor is nearing complete renewal; only a few blackened openings remain to be refurbished, filled with newly cut stone. His fortitude and perseverance alone have made this transformation possible; he has kept the workmen painstakingly on their task. A winning smile crosses his face.

From the parapet of the castle tower, he looks out across the landscape to view the vastness of the castle lands and he feel great pride. His heart leaps as he looks down upon the Knell River with its serpentine watery swirls around the rocks at the base of the cliff.

"All that I survey is mine! Castle Baine is mine!" Edmud shouts up to the shiny full moon that he is sure is listening.

"All of this is yours and mine, my sweet Kyla," proclaims Edmud, as he reaches up toward the sky... "This land, this castle, is the greatest gift I can ever give you!"

Unsteadily, Edmud inches his way across a newly laid wooden floor planks. Suddenly, a powerful queasiness grips him, a horrid nausea and the most deadly shuttering—severe and savage bolts of pain striking hard and deadly in the middle of his body. His brows flush with drops of sweat. His gut is alive with fire, the pain excruciating.

Edmud innately responds. He leans forward quickly and grabs his stomach. This quick movement causes him to teeter totter atop the open floor beams, like a trick dog losing its battle to stay on a circus ball.

Reeling from both agony and dizziness, Edmud momentarily stops. Then, abruptly, forcefully, he pitches forward, almost as if someone had shoved him—hard. With the force of a stone hurled by a catapult, he land into the stony abyss far below, with a most deadly sounding thud. Whump!

The last thought that enters Edmud's mind is his lovely vision of Kyla, smiling, because she knows that the golden coin will be returned. She gently lifts him to her bosom, as in the past; she hugs him, and strokes his hair.

Mothers often find their sons to be an albatross. The ones they have created. This happens inside. Outside... the whiskey-brown burns rush icily down from the mountains.

The idle sounds from high-pitched fifes in the green sober glen meet the singsong of far off highland fiddles.

CHAPTER TEN

Time of New Life.

Returning from the meadow, Fiona is struck with a sudden onset of abdominal pain, and she doubles over in distress and anguish. "Dear gods," she anxiously exclaims, "I fear that the time of new life has come. Help me please to my room," she pleads to Noah and Emil.

Noah seems distraught. Extremely concerned when he comes to realize that this forthcoming birth will be happening at the moment the moon waxes the sun, he activates his plan to do what he does best... helping... getting aid for the new mother to be! He intends to leave the fortress immediately after seeing to Fiona's needs, putting her in comfort to rest until he could bring Una to help with the baby's delivery.

Upon opening the door of the Fortress to head toward Una's wooden hut by the river, Noah encounters Una, standing there, right in front of him! He is aghast! He cannot believe she is at Lockmoor, a most welcomed sight... and so primed for the night's event.

"Do not be flustered, nor surprised Noah. I have waited for this day. The time of the new moon has come... the time for change and newness."

She seems quite sufficiently prepared... as if she had a sixth sense about the baby's imminent birth.

Roots of hawthorn, hastily shoved into the pockets of her dark and flowing cloak, peek out, like long tenacious green fingers, seeking first light. She speaks. "These roots will ward off anxiety... I needed to bring them. I feel our new mother-to-be is anxious about this night."

Noah reacts to her words, "You seem to be anxious about this night as well. How is it you knew to be ready?"

"I turned to the Tarot. The fate card of the II of Swords showed its face and enabled me to see precisely what will happen here today, that Fiona's time has come. I am here to help determine the outcome of this day."

Noah is awestruck with her clairvoyance.

"I am overjoyed that you are here. My mind can rest at ease," sighs Noah, hugging Una to his strong chest.

"Tonight is the night of the Witches' Sabbath," Una continues in a conversant tone. "It is a good omen. The gods have foretold that a girl child would be safely born this day."

"Then hurry!" urges Noah.

Una smiles for she knows, quite well, that she has assisted her mother, Suda, in the birthing process, be it ladies of the house, or scullery maids. She is well schooled and capable of the task at hand.

A Cause for Joy.

Within the yawning fortress, Una finds that Fiona has taken up her quarters in the lying-in room by two female servants, one older, one younger. The women have freshly swept the floor and covered it with clean, fragrant rushes. The fireplace has been lit and the room is warm. In addition to the bright fire, thirteen tall tallow candles have been lit; they glow brightly, giving the room light.

Tightly grasping Una's hand, Fiona exclaims, "You're here! Thank the gods! I am so apprehensive about this night."

"There, there, my good friend. All is well. You will deliver a healthy baby this night. Trust and believe... all will be fine, I promise you."

Una then takes charge... to the obvious displeasure of the midwives. With sheeting of blue, she masked the damp Fortress walls, cleverly creating a vast blue-sky backdrop. She has used the formula kept secret for centuries, sharing it with none. The Druids of long ago had charged into battle in chariots, often naked and painted with this same blue dye called "woad," as the color blue brings relaxation and respite.

The scent of wild flowers emanates from crystal like urns and the gentle sound of plucking harp strings fill the room—a room that has been magically transformed into a peaceful meadows... mysteriously, trees grew in hedgerows and in deep mystifying glens— half suited to the belief that fairies survive here!

She then places a greenish ragweed on Fiona's pillow, a spray that will ward off all evil spirits. From a red colored silk bag, with a drawstring closure, she produces a long golden chain. From it hangs a golden replica of an albatross. As she watches this medalled bird swing to and fro, Fiona eyes flutter and gently close. She is now in a restful twilight sleep, hopefully to remains in this hypnotic sleep until the beautiful moment of delivery. The wonder of it all!

Una tells Noah to fetch three buckets, one filled with water, one with milk, and one filled with wine, and to place them by the fireside.

Having done this, Una solemnly dictates, "Now, please Noah, leave the room and wait outside with Emil. I feel I will need your help before the night is over."

As Una moves around Fiona's birthing bed, she exhibits a strong air of confidence about the tremendous task at hand; she quite knowingly directs the two midwives who help assist her. Fiona, holding her body stiffly and resolutely, hands clench tightly to her sides, slowly relaxes.

"You will be soothed and calmed, the baby will sense this calmness," says Una, in a soft mild voice. "Just listen to my words and peacefulness will follow. Come, we will prepare you."

Una guides her, tenderly; quietly through the anguish that only one giving birth fights. The child… happily conceived… very difficult to deliver. *Have I no husband to help me through these difficult times… to hold my hand?* But that was not the way of the highlander man.

A white moist cloth that has been soaked in crushed lavender petals is softly placed onto Fiona's forehead. Una continues to pacifying Fiona in a soft soothing voice, and gently urges the young woman to relax. Removing Fiona's chemise from her body, Una partially cover her with a clean sheet of muslin. She then lowers her head to Fiona's swollen belly and listens for the sounds of the fetus within.

Looking into Fiona's dark scared eyes that show alarm, Una says, "All is well. Be calm. Your baby will be here before the moon has waned."

Placing a piece of willow bark to Fiona's lips, Una quietly instructs, "Chew on this bark when a strong sharpness comes to your loins, it will help you forget the pain."

The contractions strengthen. Una rubs Fiona's round belly with lavender ointment to lessen her pain and hasten the process of childbirth. As the evening passes, Una watching Fiona's face for signs of birthing readiness, and she quietly tells Fiona when it is time to bear down to help the miracle of birth happen.

Pain follows pain, yet Fiona endures. Her moans are monotone, barely audible. She thrashes around in the bed and rocks her head to and fro slightly… she is talking to herself: *My suffering is a release, a penance, for all the wrong deeds I have done in my life.*

Fiona mindfully experiences the powerful sensation of forgiveness, toward Steward… and from Steward… entering her soul. *Enduring the birthing of this child, conceived in love, will free me from all past evil.*

Suddenly, Fiona is jarred from her analyzing thoughts by a knife-sharp pain in her abdomen.

Una's heart begins to race; she knows that something has gone wrong. Adeptly, she applies pressure in downward strokes on Fiona's stomach in an attempt to expel the child. Una commands the two midwives to help as she pushes again and again on Fiona's abdomen. When the crowning of the baby's head occurs, Fiona bears down one last time with extreme force… and the little infant, finally separated from her mother's body, arrives in this world.

The tiny baby is blue. Una puts the baby over her knee and taps profoundly on her back. On turning her over, she breathes five short breaths into the baby's mouth. This procedure continues until the newborn finally yells out in a screech. Una hold the baby by her tiny feet and slaps her firmly on her small rounded baby buttocks. Oxygen races to her tiny lungs and a rosy color rushes to the newborn's once gray-white face. A second screech rings out --one that could be heard across the countryside.

Ah! A blissful moment! The strong cry of an infant… the heartbeat of the world.

Baby Girl.

And the tears roll silently down the cheeks and the pale face of Fiona. Tears, not of sadness, but of joy. The mystery of giving birth has been solved. Only a woman knows such inner joy and fulfillment.

She fondly turns to kiss the sweet baby face of her daughter, so delicately placed in her arms. The infant yawns, her little hands and fingers now making fists… she is ready to fight the world and its obsessions and lassitude. The baby girl, with flossy hair closely matted to her head, and eyes squeezed shut, enjoying her final destination, thru the birth canal—to life—one day to see sun, stars, and the golden face that smiles from the moon… a world of promise.

Totally unaware that she has been born under the heavenly designed stars in the Sagittarius pattern, these December stars that determine leaders of the world. Sagittarius—it is a good sign. She is destined to become a lover of people.

Coddled in silk, the sweet pink mouth, seeks out a nipple that will give her succulence. Colostrums! Nectar she would learn to love. Cute little feet already have the Highlander's need to dance... to the piper's tune... and the tweeting of the tin whistle.

And what does the world offer this child? Hopefully—a time to sing—a time to dream 'neath the gold of the moon! In a quiet dream state, the baby smiles.

This baby girl—only minutes old—senses her importance—and sucks on her fingers—knowing she will be a princess. The Fortress, or "caer," gives way to this day of celebration. The princess of Lockmoor and Castle Baine has arrived!

Readiness.

Only Una knows the importance of a speedy Baptism. The baby was born blue-- the midwives mistakenly thought that meant she would be a regal child. In all actuality, the baby's heart had stopped.

Una smilingly faces her two assistants, and says in a voice filled with happiness, and heartfelt concern. "I think it is best that the Baptismal ceremony take place at this time. We must give thanks that all has been accomplished here this night, and ask that the protection of the gods be brought upon the child. But first, our strong, tiny baby girl is to be cleansed for the blessings she is about to receive."

The two women take the infant and cleanse her in a small tub of wine, mixed with rose petals. One servant then washes the baby's tongue with cooling water, assuring that she will speak properly, and, next, putting sweet honey on her finger, she gently rubs the inside of the baby's mouth in the hopes of giving the baby a splendid appetite.

As the women examine the infant's body, the baby seems perfect in every way, little feet, little hands that were meant to reach for her mother's face. Upon washing the baby's back, they are slightly alarmed to see a small red mark on the baby's shoulder. The "birthmark" has the appearance of the sign of the cross; the cross is a perfect red "t."

Seeing this, the older servant raises her finger to her lips, giving a motion for silence, softly whispers to the other woman, "Hush."

The infant girl, happily snuggled and swaddled under white linen strips so that her legs might grow straight and strong, is laid in a wooden cradle in the darkest segment of the room, so her eyes will be protected from the bright blaze of the fireplace.

The midwives had heard quite enough of this already rambunctious baby. Knowing that all is finally peaceful, the servants ready the room for the baptism.

They cleanse away all signs of what has transpired this night. Eradicating all signs of womanly blood and pain… and miracles.

The Knowing.

Bundling up the soiled linens, the women make their way to the washroom. As they head down the passageway, the older biddy, with a slight head gesture, indicating upstairs, asks: "Was that not the strangest sight to see?"

The younger one nods in agreement. "And what should we be doing?"

"Bite your tongue... for your own safekeeping. Speak of what has happened here to no one."

"And who would believe us if we were to tell them?" The younger servant rattles on, still indignant about the way Una had taken control of the evening.

"Harp music, hypnosis, a blue baby, all that folderol and magic. If you ask me, when the birth did not come within 20 contractions, the black haired witch should have set Noah and Emil to open all the cupboards and all of the drawers, untie knots, and unlock chests... to help bring the baby into the world!" The younger woman stammers on in a knowing manner, looking toward her mentor for approval.

"Or she could have sent Emil into the courtyard to shoot an arrow at the night's full moon! This is what we would have done to bring the baby out! These highland practices have always worked before!" the older woman adds, with a sly grin.

"When Una placed a poultice on Fiona's abdomen to help her heal... and put a drop of the child's blood on the mother's lips... to promote bonding... I thought I was going to die! Too much witchcraft for me... Spooky!"

"And that poor wee one has been marked with the sign of the devil! Marked by Steward… that no good evil man!" the all-knowing older woman spouts. "I have never seen the likes of this before!"

"Mark my word, as well," adds her apprentice. "That was truly a sign of the cross on her back, the poor little thing! Evil is truly crossing over from the land of lost souls to that baby girl, this day. I think the baby is cursed… cursed, I tell you!"

She receives an explosive reprimand from her cohort. "Hush now! Keep your silly claptrap shut or I will have to take a bloody shovel to your head!"

The younger girl is totally silenced.

The elder bitty completes her warning. "Do not speak of this night to anyone for your own good… and mine. Best forget all we have seen here before that silly black witch plops a deadly curse on us!"

CHAPTER ELEVEN

The Celebration.

This is an eve of celebration. Primarily, the princess of Lochmoor and Castle Baine has arrived. But secondly, it is the feast of the Winter Solstice—a special time in an eclipse when the sun apparently stands still in its northward and southward motion.

According to the Celts sacred dictates, the Baptism of a child born on the Eve of the revered Winter Solstice must be performed before the moonlit night turns into the light of day. Time is of the essence.

The main Hall is brightly bedecked in evergreens of mistletoe—cut from their growing place on the hallowed oak—with thickly clustered leaves, waxy white berries, and small yellow flowers, which send pastel shards of palest color capering across the large room, reflecting the light of the slowly burning peat fires aglow in the giant fireplace.

The men in the fortress are quite delighted. Time to bring forth the entire stash of liquid libation one could lay one's hands on. From the catacombs of the fortress, the eager participants begin to gather—from animal groom to soldier, cooks to menial servants, horse trainer to herder—and the festivities commence.

The call, "'Tis time to raise some grouse!" festers.

The Baptism.

Una takes the strong and healthy, screaming infant from her cradle, and places her in Fiona's arms. She asks Fiona what name she has chosen for the child by which she will be identified throughout her life.

Fiona responds, "Miah, for the flowers of the field"... as she thinks back momentarily about the heather covered meadows of Lockmoor... and her first true love.

Putting salt into the mouth of the baby to represent the reception of wisdom, Una exorcises any demons, saying, "Na deithe libh, (Gods be with you)."

Taking a small container of oil, she pours a tiny amount on her thumb, and makes a sign of the cross first on the baby's forehead and then on the baby's chest, saying, "I anoint you, Miah, with oil for strength."

Holding high a cup of water, Una chants, "An uisco seo, (behold the waters of life)."

The baby is anointed with the water as a sign of purity, and a small amount of the liquid is poured over the infant's head, as she lay cradled in Fiona's arms.

"From this moment forward, you will be known as Miah, daughter of Fiona, heir to Castle Baine."

Una asks of Fiona, "Who will be the guardians for your daughter?"

With a good sense of satisfaction and love in her voice, Fiona declares that Noah and Emil will be Miah's guardians "to help kindle the sacred fire of wisdom, love, and power within the child and keep her out of harm's way."

As Una ties the red string bracelet, an amulet, onto Miah's wrist, the baby's little hand suddenly reaches out... almost as if in understanding of the love that surrounds her.

Una concludes, "May the child be safely guarded and protected through her lifetime by Noah and Emil. Go raibh beannacht Na ndeithe agus ar sinsir ar Mio, (May the Gods and ancestors bless Miah)."

All are full of joy and contentment on this night of the Witches' Sabbath.

One Task Remains.

Una's work is not yet done; one major task remains to be completed before she rests: she must take the placenta, which has been wrapped in the muslin cloth from the birthing bed, to the meadow, and bury it, covertly. And this she does with the help of Noah. Determined, the pair tore out into the night.

Now well past midnight, they enter the meadow of Lockmoor in search of Steward's grave. The moon was a perfect circle, so full of light that all the edges of things had an amber cast. The full moon above acts as both a blessing and a curse; the moon lights their way but allows others to witness their mission.

Una directs Noah to dig a hole to the right of the gallan (standing stone) marking the grave. As the cloth sack is placed in the shallow grave, Una pours a cup of ale around the ritual space and asks that the forces of the dark be turned away from this child's path of life, and may the forces of evil be now appeased.

She chants, "May the spirit of good, which comes in light, thrice bless the way of this newborn baby. May the gods be pleased with the birth of Miah this night. May she also gain the strength to endure all ill will cast upon her, and have the blessing of earth, fire, and water to kill off all evil demons. Biodh se amhlaidh, (So be it)."

Heir to the Castle.

In a matter of days, a lone boat ties up to the moorings of the Fortress. Fighting the swift and changing currents of the Knell, dodging the shaggy rocks of the shoreline is a task that demands much prowess and maneuverings with the rudder. The bearer of bad tidings has come in with the tide.

Each new birth brings with it a new death. The giving and the taking away. The cold rainfall of the morning will now fall in droplets into the lives of many.

The messenger is made to wait while the mistress of the house is ready to receive him.

This envoy rushes to Lockmoor, tromps over the moat, to tell his news: the sudden death of Edmud.

The man is exhausted from the trip and filled with anxiety. "Our Lord Edmud had broken his neck in a fall from the east tower of Castle Baine," he urgently reports to Fiona, who is strangely saddened upon hearing the shocking and deadly news.

The messenger continues his babbling. "His broken body was found by two of the guards who discovered his remains amidst the rocks and the stony debris that lies at the base of the tower. They carried his rigid corpse into the Great Hall. He was placed on a wooden pallet so he could be watched through the night for signs that life may come back to his rigid body.

One servant thrust a sharp needle into his big toe to see if he responded to the pain. This vigil proved fruitless as no breath… no whimper… did escape his mouth. Edmud was truly dead. Dead as a doornail!"

"What is it you wish from me?" asked Fiona in a controlled, thin voice.

"I am sorry to be the bearer of such grim news, but I am here to tell of good news also. We have learned that you and your infant daughter are now heirs to Castle Baine, as you are the bride… and Miah is the daughter of Steward," proclaimed the messenger, his voice gaining strength.

Upon hearing this, Fiona's heart almost leaped out of her body. "Such jubilant news indeed," mused Fiona, as the words, "Heir to the castle," rocked her very being. A message she has long awaited.

There is a gleam of exhilarating delight in Fiona's eye as she pleads for the man to continue.

"But my task is two fold. We need your approval regarding the burial ritual," the man explained.

"There are plans afoot to proceed with the death practices due a nobleman. As of now, Edmud's body has been washed and then dressed in his finest tunic. He has been wrapped in a white linen shroud and placed in a six-sided wedge shaped coffin of pine. The coffin has been draped with the red and gold banner of Castle Baine and remains in the Great Hall of the castle," the man said in a voice seeking approval for all these completed tasks.

"I ask again, what is it you wish from me?" questioned Fiona, her mind racing wildly.

"We need to know what to do next... and who will be in charge of the castle 'til your arrival... given your frail condition at the moment... with a newly born baby... and all," the messenger stammers on.

Fiona ponders this request momentarily, and responds quite boldly. "Until that time I can travel north to Castle Baine, I will send two of my most trusted men with you to help complete Edmud's burial arrangement. I will instruct them as to Edmud's final resting place. These men will organize the castle guards and servants of the household until my arrival 40 days hence. It is then we will celebrate the Sharoke, the final ceremony for Edmud, that will release his spirit from the castle to the land of the dead."

Fiona has thoughtfully set her plan into motion.

CHAPTER TWELVE

Forty-Day Wait.

Summoning Noah and Emil, Fiona tells them of her plans. They are to leave the fortress and travel to Castle Baine.

Speaking to Emil, Fiona says, "Emil, you are wise to the ways of the nobles, being the son of a true landowner yourself, and you know what is expected of you as you lead the servants and guards to remain honorable to Castle Baine. I thereby give you the power to act in my behalf... and for baby Miah. You are entrusted to keep Castle Baine safe from all who might intrude at this time of mourning."

"As you wish," Emil says. "But I am glad that Noah is traveling with me to the castle as his fighting power is well known throughout this land. There will be peace in the castle, guaranteed."

"There is another task for you, Emil," continues Fiona. "As is the burial practice, I trust you to search for something valuable that belonged to Edmud, or perhaps a piece of Kyla's jewelry or a resplendent gem, to be placed in Edmud's casket, to calm and quiet his spirit. Choose wisely."

"This I can do," he responds.

"I know you will chose wisely, Emil. Make sure, as well, that Edmud has a proper burial. Position his coffin so it faces to the East. We need his spirit to be welcomed in the land of the dead, not to be wildly roaming around the passageways of Castle Baine!"

Within the granted forty days, Fiona readies for her trip to Castle Baine, knowing the urgency of time and the need for the ritual of the Sharoke ceremony for Edmud. And, more significantly, she must be wholly prepared to take over as Lady of Castle Baine!

She journeys north across the frozen dirt roads in a caravan complete with a band of guards, baby Miah, who is wrapped snuggly in fur blankets, the baby's nurse, and her trusted and faithful friend, Una. Upon arrival at Baine, Fiona notes the darkness of this vast estate—all in darkness—but more than that—their eerie echoes convey death and foreboding.

Emil readily concurs. He is most anxious to report of the strange and macabre events of the last several weeks.

Emil tells his story, leaving out no detail.

"One was not prepared for the burial ceremony in the Great Hall. The night of the burial, every candle was lit to change the dark demure of the room to one of light that would be welcome to the angels of grace. The wake began on a rather dismal note, but then the drinking began… and the servants and guards began to sing… almost joyously. It was as if all were convinced of the thought, that they, too, might be the next victims of death and the dark beyond. They seemed intent on finding happiness today," says Emil.

As he mused philosophically to himself, Emil nods his head in understanding. *"Their thoughts are true… No one knows when his or her time of reckoning will come… Life is short… Yes… life is very short."*

"Edmud's body was buried in the grave site beyond the castle," Emil continues on, "next to the standing stone that tells the story of Lady Kyla, his stepmother. A mound of earth covers his burial place, and his grave is marked with five large stones."

After a long pause of a moment or two, maybe more, Emil's face turns dark and serious; he warns, "But all is not safe here."

Emil recounts, in a whisper, more of the ghostly happenings of Castle Baine.

"Many eerie events occurred after that burial night. The people of the household reportedly saw a rachitic old man mounted on a skeletal gelding riding throughout the castle, soundlessly, as if in search of something lost."

"One scared servant reported that he saw a banshee, with her huge nostril emitting gray smoke... her long red hair streaming behind her... whining... wailing... running through the dark rooms of the tower in the wee hours of the morning; he was frightened to death. Ghosts and mysterious shadows have been seen in the passageways. There truly is much unrest here."

Talk of ghouls and grave robbers...

"Is it possible to put Edmud's spirit to rest so he will no longer terrorize and frighten the living?" asked Emil, shaking his head in quandary.

"I did everything you ordered, Fiona. I placed a valuable pearl necklace of Lady Kyla's in his casket. What more was I to do?"

A Possible Solution.

"Perhaps it is the ghost of Edmud roaming through the night in search of something... something he values… something he cannot leave behind in the world of the living. We must help him find what he seeks, and bury it in his grave," Fiona resolves.

"In the ceremony of the Sharoke, perhaps Una will discover what it is that Edmud is searching for in the castle. Hopefully, Edmud will give us a sign, and a clue, as to the whys and wherefores that trouble him. I know he will give us peace in exchange for our aid. If we help him find what it is he is searching for… his spirit will have rest." Heads of the listening nod in accord.

The Sharoke.

The Sharoke is held on the cool morn marking the fortieth day since the death of Edmud of Castle Baine. A few hours after sunrise, a thick white mist rises and blankets the land. These white misty billows, shrouds for reality, seem to be guarding the spirits of the dead.

The cemetery was a quadroon set apart on the western valley of the castle by pillars of stone and hand-forged metal, offering the ancient dead some peace. The buried were said to be able to warm their bones in the light of the unleashed sun as it rose each day in dull light of morning in the eastern sky.

Una, Emil, Noah, a smattering of faithful servants, and Fiona have gathered together in stillness at Edmud's burial plot near to the standing stone of Lady Kyla.

A few of the guards and servant of the household have willingly joined in the event; some attended out of fear of reprisals from Edmud's spirit, as they continue to harbor bitter feelings toward him because of his unkind treatment over the last few months, and yet, a few have come to simply celebrate and drink the wine. All join together in a semicircle facing Edmud's shallow grave as the ritual of the Sharoke commences.

Una begins by lighting of the tine choisricthe (Sacred fire) at the foot of Edmud's stone covered resting place. She invites in the gods, the dead, and the power of the spirits, and chants.

"I summon the power of earth, air, water, and fire, (Yala onna en' kemen, en' vilya, en' alu, and en' naur), gather with us here this day to peacefully welcome the spirit of Edmud into the land of dead. Come Druids all, and let your minds be still, as the gods reveal their will."

All in attendance respond, "Biodh se (be it so)."

Una's voice continues, "Today is the fortieth day of forgiving and completion to clear the way for peace of the spirit of this man. Gods, give us an earthly sign if there is some deed that we must do before Edmud's spirit can cross over to the land of the dead before this day is done."

"You will reach us, you will teach us, and reveal our task of fate," chants Una.

The offering to the gods and the dead is sealed with the words, "By fire and well, by sacred tree, give us a sign of the offering we can make to ye."

The group repeats in unison, "Biodh se (be it so)."

To conclude the ritual, the gods are asked to open the gates so Edmud's spirit of life will be free to find peace with the spirits of his ancestors.

Una chants, "Osclaitear na geatai (Let the gates be opened)."

The cool winds of the highlands carry her melodious voice to high and low lands, across the rugged landscape.

All reply, "Biodh se."

Noah, listening attentively to the final atonement, finds his mind suddenly straying. He is thinking that a body is supposed to stay beneath the earth... and how happy and satisfied he will be when Edmud is finally put to rest.

"It is time for Edmud's spirit to stop thinking outside the box, the pine box," his inner voice whispers.

The day turns cool and friendly. The mist is dissipating, moving away in search of another valley, strath or glen, to haunt and pester. Above, the sky is blue and cloudless.

Following the Sharoke, the servants help spread out a large white cloth on the rugged ground and set down huge dishes of various foods--veal, mutton, simmering in their juices--and jugs of wine so that those in attendance can toast Edmud's day of crossing over to the spirit world. All participants appear cheerful, albeit jolly, as they drink and sup heartily, in the hope that this day will soon end... and Edmud's spirit will leave the castle forever!

Midst the celebration, a cool gust of wind begins to blow through green shade trees that stand tall and stately over the head of the marked graves. The wind is not threatening, but rather kind and melodious.

However, all stand motionless, now hearing the sound of bells-- tinkling bells, chiming softly in a series of small, short, light tolls, like those of a very small cymbal. The sound lasts momentarily, and the workers blithely return to their food feast and gossiping about the strangeness of the day.

But Fiona realizes that the message of the bells is meant for her... and her alone! The solution to ridding herself of Edmund's ghost lies within her own being... within her power.

The Search is Ended.

"I can give the golden coin of Augustalis back to Edmud," Fiona decides at last.

"This coin has been the bane of my existence since I first laid eyes on it the night before my wedding. Besides, there must be many more riches in the castle that are now mine and Miah's to share. This exchange is only fair, for all that Edmud has promised me."

Hasty plans to have Noah bury the coin down in the dirt of Edmud's grave this very day, before the rising of the moon, are set into motion.

"Be gone, spirits of Edmud... and let the dead bury the dead," Fiona pronounces with firmness of mind.

"Peace will prevail if the coin is never disturbed from its final resting place," Una hastily warns. Dark eyes indicate the seriousness of what she says.

That night at the castle is a most quiet one, indeed. No shrieks of wailing banshees... no screeching from the dark castle towers. If the truth be known, most of the servants, fearing hoodoo, slept the night under the covers, with their fingers crossed!

"If a few shadows remain, so be it. They can be dealt with. The power of a dead man's spirit will be ended on this very day," promises Fiona with a fleeting half smile.

Early the next morning, Fiona and Noah visit the grave of Edmud, only to find, to their wonder and amazement, that the pile of five stone, once mounted on top the grave mound, has been systematically rearranged into the sign of a small cross, simulation to a "T."

"'Twas not I that has made this sign of the cross!" Noah says in a defensive tone. "Could it be the work of the spirit world?"

"Has Edmud truly succeeded in crossing over to the nether land of the dead... or will his spirit come back to haunt us, me and my baby?" thinks Fiona, who, at the moment, fearfully examines these questions in her mind.

Is it now a cosmic air that chills her spine...

So shall your reap! So shall you sow!

CHAPTER THIRTEEN

Farewell Warning.

As Una prepares to leave Castle Baine to return to her small hut in the green forest beyond Lockmoor, she speaks to Fiona and presents this conundrum. "Do you think it all ends with bones in the ground? You can never be certain that a spirit has passed into the world of the dead."

Fiona listens attentively as Una proceeds with her warning, as her dire wish is to find a true sense of safety in the castle.

"There are measures you can take to protect yourself and baby Miah from the demons of this castle. First, do not rattle the living that work here. If you are going to make changes, make them simple. You must keep the servants on your side. Secondly, above all, keep the tables... the chairs... the candlesticks... in their set places. Do not move or re-hang the tapestries or the paintings."

"Touch nothing?" quizzes Fiona, her eyes narrowing with concern. "Oh, my stars!"

"You must realize that for the ghost... if there should be a ghost... everything must be kept exactly as it was while he or she was alive. Ghosts delight when they come and visit a familiar past... and you may be having visitors."

Fiona, although addled by the thought of ghostly guests, albeit uninvited, nods her head in understanding; she cannot help praying, *Ghosts, be gone!*

Una carefully ties an amulet made of dried senna, mint, and rue around Fiona's wrist and orders Fiona not to remove the bracelet, as it will help cast away all evil here at Castle Baine.

"You must stay calm and unruffled. If strange happenings occur, if weird sounds are heard in the night, any bump, any bang, any howl of a banshee, you must be the strong example to all others here at the castle. Remember, the gods have the power to protect you and baby Miah. If you believe that the gods will give you strength to endure… it will be done. You must believe!"

Una clasps Fiona's hands in hers and prays the prayer of the Shaman.

"Spirits of the tree, the bile, the crann, give Fiona inner strength; spirits of the fire, well, and earth, guide her. Goddess of the Hearth, beat powerful and pure in the heart of this woman. God of the four borders, north, south, east, and west, stand ready to repulse all disorder from this castle and bring peace."

Reaching out to make the sign of the circle of the gods—the shape of the moon—on Fiona's forehead, Una concludes her requests, "Go raibh beannacht ar sinsir ar Fiona. May the gods bless Fiona. Biodh se amhlaidh, so be it!"

Seeing Una and Noah set out for Lockmoor, fear and apprehension flash through Fiona. "I am alone and in charge of Castle Baine."

She takes a wistful breath. "I must succeed!" "No. I will succeed! So be it!" she proclaims.

Alone at the Castle.

Morning has broken. Fiona awakens in absolute awe of surviving her first dark dream filled night. She quickly reaches under her down filled pillow to retrieve the seven light blue beads, strung together with Celtic knots, a fetish, legendary in warding off dark evil, given to her by Una.

"Spirit of the fetish, I am grateful that you have protected me from all eerie shadows and ghosts… the ghosts of Steward, Edmud, and Kyla, who may be lurking outside the castle walls… or hiding in any dim cobwebbed corner… ready to do harm, to strike at any given moment."

"Yes," Fiona concludes her thoughts. "Three bodies rotting in their crypts, buried outside the castle gates now, but I cannot say for certain that three spirits will stay put under the dirt of their freshly drug graves."

Unable to dismiss this ominous feeling that she is not alone in the castle… this stony citadel that rocks with evil… Fiona vows to triumph as Lady of the castle. "No! I will not fail at the exigent tasks that lie before me."

I must force these morose and morbid thoughts out of my restless mind. I must take charge… and save my sanity.

Fearful as a young child lost in a maze, Fiona calls out.

"Spirits of the universe, I believe! I believe you can make me strong. Guide me on the path to healing waters. Wash all my torment away." Her tears take up the challenge.

A Castle Day.

Foremost, Fiona must see to baby Miah, sleeping contentedly in the adjoining bedchamber. The sweet baby, tucked away in her little cradle, sleeps under the critical eyes of her wet nurse, the baby's constant companion... the young woman chosen by Fiona to suckle the hungry child as Fiona's breasts are barren of mother's milk.

Fiona awakens Miah gently with soft words. "Hush, little baby... Mum is here."

In the early morning hour, this young mother sings lullabies to the wee one in a quiet voice, *"Hush little Miah, say not a word, I am going to buy you a golden bird."*

Sometimes, she may simply whisper the pleasant tales she had heard at her own mother's knee. Tales of the land... the evergreen wooded forest... the silvery shining River Knell... and she gently hugs the little baby to her heart.

In return, little Miah reaches her tiny hands up to her mother's face and knowingly grabs at her mother's long brown hair, making Fiona laugh with delight. These cherished moments are kept in Fiona's heart as the two rock peacefully together in the large oaken rocking chair, the wedding chair... purposely brought here from Lockmoor.

Meanwhile, the baby's nurse has risen from her truckle bed, has washed and dressed herself, and pushed her bed out of sight behind its curtains. When the maidservant brings an ewer, a large water pitcher, of warm water from the kitchen for Miah's bath, Fiona is pleased to place the baby in the nurse's arms, content in the knowing that the infant is in reliable, loving hands.

Fiona's second major duty is to address the trials and tribulations… and the antics of the household workers of the castle. She must acclimate herself to castle conditions… and directly discovers that castle demands are far more rigid and grueling than the free-spirited life she was accustomed to at Lockmoor.

As the Lady of the house, Fiona is completely in charge of the daily routines, simple or complex, and she controls all of the decisions, major or minor, that affect the entirety of the castle life, a seriously stressful responsibility. She must oversee the work of the household servants and supervise the dairy… the gardens… the kitchen… the whole lot!

A stringent routine is the only way to survive successfully… I must keep a watchful eye on everyone!

At dawn at Castle Baine, the watchman sounds a horn from the battlements of the keep to announce the noisy attack on the day. By five o'clock, the castle is a bustle of activity. Breakfast of little more than bread and ale is served in the Great Hall without ceremony. Then the obligatory chores of the day begin.

After mucking out the stalls, making it clean for the fastidiously fussy horses, the Thoroughbreds and Hackneys alike, the workers must wheelbarrow the manure to the vegetable and flower gardens, put oats in the hanging mangers for the horses, feed the chickens, peafowl, and pigeons, groom and shoe the horses, polish the carriages so they are ready to travel at a moment's notice, and clean the courtyard of any rubbish or rubble.

The hard working female servants have their morning chores within the castle walls. They clean and polish the pewter and silver plates and goblets till they shine. They spin. They weave. They sew all the clothing of the household, from fine linen underwear to outer garments woven with gold and silver or trimmed with squirrel fur.

Three cooks, continually bantering and babbling as they work in the small kitchen, prepare the midday meal, which is served between nine and eleven each morning. The din is raucous with the rattling of pots and pans, sounding like a team of armored knights in the midst of battle.

The choice of meal, be it poultry or fish, cheese or eggs, rabbit or deer, must be selected by Fiona, who holds the only key to the larder and to the buttery where all the priceless food supplies... the verjuice (a sour juice squeezed from crab apples)... the wine... the liquor... the salted meats... are stored behind securely bolted and locked doors, safe from the greedy and grasping hands of any thieving servant.

With every jingle-jangle of these invaluable keys... the keys to the kingdom... the keys to life... that she wears around her now slim waist, Fiona is reminded of the enormous burden she has taken upon her shoulders.

"Gods, give me strength to endure this day," she pleads.

Fiona is cordial toward the servants, as she was duly advised. She does not want to have the workers regress back to their feelings of animosity toward the Lady of the house, as in the past; she hopes to make a difference by listening to their concerns regarding their grueling and exhausting jobs.

The task will be difficult to resolve, at best. Fiona must proceed with caution, she admits, as these workers are a tough crew of rag tag people, vagabonds and rogues, or so Emil, who had observed their antics over the last 40 days, has reported. Knowing full well that "old ways die hard," Fiona seeks to gain their trust; she must have the workers pledge their allegiances to Castle Baine… *"Yes, my Lady,"* would be sweet music to her ears.

But needless to say, the servants continue their insidious complaining and squabbling amongst themselves. With the passing of each day, a disgruntled servant chooses to tattletale to Fiona, reporting, "The other servants are not doing their fair share of the work. I deserve a second bowl of pottage, thick vegetable soup, at supper, for the labors I have done this day."

And Fiona sits and listens intensively… trying to resolve each individual's complaint. *Oh god, help me to be fair… help me solve the puzzle!*

Treasure.

In contrast, Fiona is joyously content about her riches, even if she must learn how to deal with her newly acclaimed trove of treasures. It took but one trip up the dim passageway to the musty treasury room in the west tower to make Fiona realize she has stepped into another world.

"Oh, my little Miah, we have inherited a prosperous, wealthy castle, indeed."

Upon opening the tightly tied leather bags of gleaming gold and silver coins, and the wooden chest filled with fine jewels and precious stones, shiny silver cups, and pewter candlesticks, Fiona is so grandly ecstatic over her rich fate that she cannot resist dancing merrily around the coffers of gold. Dancing, dancing, twirling, twirling... until she is breathless.

Also waltzing in the shadows... just out of sight... are the demons of moral scruples.

Little does Fiona realize that her little jig for joy will soon manifest itself into a common daily practice, as she acquiesces to her desire for riches... and the amazing things riches can bring.

"Yes," says Fiona, "Wealth... brings power and control... I cannot wait to see if these bejeweled trinkets can work magic for me... and lift the dark curtain of my future!"

A Rich Life.

"The gods have blessed me richly," declares Fiona. She vows, at that moment, to be ever faithful to the gods who have given her this opulent opportunity at a new life as Lady of Castle Baine.

To keep the castle in prosperous working order, Fiona signs newly written agreements with the various vassals leasing the surrounding farming and grazing fields for a minimal fee, in exchange for their supply of fresh meat and vegetables to the household. These tenants consent, albeit reluctantly, to aid in defending the castle against fierce attacks... by rough gangs of quick thieves... or bands of hoodlum bandits, out and about, ever ready to pillage any rich landowners, and take away each valuable bauble or bead they can lay their avaricious hands on.

Castle Guards.

Fiona plans to take stronger measures to keep Castle Baine's defenses in good order, as she has learned that the two greedy Averys, noblemen to the east, owners of the land between Castle Baine and Fortress Lockmoor... down river on the powerful Knell, are ready to pick a quarrel or make a sudden attack upon any neighbor, at any given time, at any given moment... and that neighbor could be her, especially if these bold men are desirous of gaining more land, her land... and gaining the power that land ownership brings with it.

Captain of the Guards.

To defend against this looming threat, Fiona calls on Emil's help once again. She places him in charge of the guards and the newly hired men-at-arms, the garrison of men who gladly agree to serve Fiona for good pay, eatable food, and fair treatment. These young and eager fighting knights cross swords and promise to protect the castle from all wrongdoers, from portcullis to stone walls, from east tower to west tower, and every inch of the castle domain that lies in-between.

Emil is ever gladdened with being selected as captain of the guards; he now has the opportunity to be at Fiona's side, for almost every hour of every day.

"I am grateful for this important position," responds Emil, choosing his words wisely.

"Having lived among the nobles of the north, I know of their ruthfulness. I am honored that I will be ever present to answer your needs… and to protect you and baby Miah from all that would cause distress or harm."

This said, Emil bends one knee to the floor, takes Fiona's hand in his, and lightly brushes his lips to the back of her hand, saying, "Thank you, my Lady. It is my honor to continue to serve you."

Nights at the Castle.

The hired help are frequently frightened by the things that go bump or bang in the night… the unexplainable sounds and mysterious noises… heard in the castle after they have bedded down for the evening after a hard day's work.

"This poltergeist intruder must be identified," vows Fiona, " I must face up to him… or her. But for now, we will make it through… with the help of the gods… one night at a time."

"*There is so much to do here,*" sighs Fiona. She constantly questions how she will find the right answers to the myriad of problems that lie before her. At the very least, she must keep the workers fed…their stomachs quiet! And, most critically, she must keep all frightening and fearsome ghosts at bay!

Dusk Gathers.

Soon the light of day turns into night's darkness. Each evening after supper, Fiona spends time with baby Miah, rocking the child into a safe sleep. Late evenings, Fiona sits, all alone in a room filled with shadows. In front of the roaring peat fire of the Great Hall, she seeks warmth for her weary bone to ward off her chills; some caused by the problems of the day… some by her fear of the dark.

To relieve her overwhelming sense of self doubt, she begins the habit of braiding and re-braiding her long silken brown hair in a frugal attempt to keep her hands busy… her mind still. She can feel her imagination start to run wild as she fantasizes about her unsettling dread of black dreams. Will she be caught in the middle of a nightmare? Can she fight the troublesome night?

On clear evenings, the sky, fierce with stars, looks down, as if it knows her sadness. On stormy eves, Fiona would stand in the courtyard, watching the silver lightning streak across the black sky, listening for the rolling thunder warnings of a rising storm. Will the rains come? Can the rain wash away her tears?

Ultimately… sadly… she comes to one conclusion… she stands alone in the world, and she alone must resolve her own trials and tribulations. *This is my journey… alone…*

"May I have the protection of the Gods on me, (Cosaint n ndeithe do me)," she cries into the lone night.

Oft times, with the rising of the moon, Fiona chooses to search for Emil for company, secretly, away from the gossiping tongues of the suspicious servants, those scalawags who might spread rumors throughout the castle for their own devious pleasure... at her expense.

Emil, a familiar face... a familiar body.

The two would prattle of old times together... old youthful adventures... old plans... new fears. Caught in a vortex of ifs, she questions him. "What would I do if I didn't have you, Emil? ... If you weren't here to help me?"

Emil understands. "We have been though so much together... you and I. I will not leave you now. You must stay resolved. Put away your childish fears, Fiona."

"You are right! She retorts, her sparkling eyes ignited with resolve.

"Remind yourself that you are a chosen one; the gods do protect you at every turn. You have seized the day. Seize the night as well. Find peace."

"Peace?" questions Fiona.

Emil grabs Fiona by the shoulders and stares deep into her golden eyes. "Being the master of Castle Baine will bring you peace. You should know that! You would have stopped at nothing to get this rich piece of the highlands."

To his amazement, she admits that he knows her well. And yes, she was justifiably proud of the castle and its lands.

"Owning this land keeps me sane... and the dark forces at bay." A quiet smile crosses her lips.

"I love the land like a man loves a woman." She pauses momentarily... "With the same intensity and passion."

"The earth is a cold lover," Emil interjects. Perhaps you should seek a warm one."

Their bodies came together as Emil held her in his strong arms. Fiona welcomed the gesture.

CHAPTER FOURTEEN

Springtime.

Spring brings light and liveliness to the highlands as the shafts of sun slice through bruised winter clouds. Moist winds from the Gulf Stream warm the western coast. Heavy rains revisit the countryside, urging it green and fresh for the black-faced sheep that graze in the round, smooth, uplands. Narrow glens, and broad, rolling straths are bursting with the purple haze of heather. Fields of yellow flowers brighten the watery meadows, misty in the sun. Life begins anew.

At Castle Baine, surprisingly, come Spring, only one servant, at best, two, choose to leave the household, afraid to their wit's end by the many unexplainable, almost nightly, disturbances out and about the castle—from eerie ghostly moans to the sounds of banshees washing the clothes of the next person doomed to die. One servant complains to Fiona that the hallway candles are being mysterious extinguished on many an evening.

"This is an omen of bad things, very bad things to come, my Lady... and I do not want to be chased though the dark passageways... wearing only my night shirt... by a mischievous spirit who is up to no good."

Yet, the rest of the hardy stock of workers chose to stay on. It seems they would rather endure the frightful castle ghosts with coins jingling in their pocket then give in to their superstitions—penniless.

Fiona's is more than pleased she has survived the first cold and blustery winter at Castle Baine with all of its trivialities, ghostly and practical. The wheat, which had been harvested for the farm animals, was enough to last through the last four cold months; the ripe vegetables and apples of the fall that had been picked, pickled, and served each dinner, are only just now reaching the bottoms of their barrels. Of course there are plenty of fresh fish... succulent striped bass and rainbow trout... waiting to be caught daily in the waters of the River Knell, then cooked and salted, and brought to the table most evenings. All is good. All is well. The gods have watched over her.

The smells of the castle have not faired nearly as well as the food supply—the castle has a problem feeling green and clean. Dusty and dingy air within the castle walls has grown so nasty, foul, and offensive to human nostrils that most folk are happy to vacate the castle during the much-awaited Summer Progress, the designated time set aside for Spring cleaning.

There is much work to be done. It seems that dropped scraps of food, spilled bits of garbage, and deposits of feces left by the hunting dogs, all lie buried beneath the soiled rushes of the cavernous Great Room, causing a very wicked and vile aroma. This filth must be cleaned up and shoveled out so that fresh rushes, dried flowers, and sweet grasses can be laid down anew on freshly washed floors... hopefully changing the room's stench from bad to good again.

"Yes," Fiona muses. "A chance for change. Like the seasons... changing from spring to summer... bringing the winds from the North Sea... calming them, gently calming them."

125

"Like the flowers of the field... the purple heather... choosing now to raise their faces to bid a good day to the sunshine. In their warmth of summer, they dance to the salted mist from the sea and sway in unison, beneath blue skies and white billowing clouds."

But she is quickly brought back to reality when she spies ill-omened dark clouds in the distance... humorless clouds... clouds that gather and wait.

"Are these clouds bringing evil? Are they fraught with dangerous warnings?"

Summer Progress.

During this short cleaning season, Fiona plans to escape the trials and tribulations of Castle Baine and move on to Lockmoor Fortress for some peace of mind, and some calmness... for a few weeks. For safety sake, she will travel with a small caravan, hoping to go across the thirty miles that separate Castle Baine and Lockmoor Fortress in one full day's ride. Accompanying Fiona will be her beloved child, Miah, the baby's nurse, a few of the trusted household workers, of course, Emil, and several of his armed men, who will guard them, as they traverse, against highwaymen and thieves... or perhaps help push the wheels of the carriages out of the oozy muck and mire of the well traveled dirt roads, wet from spring rains.

During Summer Progress, no one even thinks about being without the comfort on this short hiatus away from home. So, as is the practice, Fiona plans to load one large cart with some choice amenities from the castle, including pewter dishes, silver candlesticks, the baby's cradle, and the ever-prized oaken rocking chair. Special hunting dogs and favored riding horses will be brought along, as well, least the thrill of the hunt be missed while away from the castle grounds.

Escape to Lockmoor.

In route, Fiona hopes to stop and barter at the marketplace. Special items for the larder of the Fortress, including picked foods and the spices of pepper, cinnamon, and nutmeg, and a surprise gift or two for Noah are to be purchased. She looks forward, immensely, to spending time with this honest man, who has been more than ably guarding the fortress in her absence.

Fiona can't wait to confer with her dear friend, Una, about some of the "goings on" and gossip at Castle Baine… and simply, to sit and talk to someone she can trust, to tell of her fears of the ghosts who haunt the castle. Fiona also desperately needs Una to concoct some herbal medicines to remedy baby Miah's persistent whooping cough, one that kept all awake throughout the long winter nights at the castle, and worries Fiona no end.

Perhaps I can find a gold or silver trinket at the fair… a present for Una… a gift that will let her know how much I need her as my friend and confident, Fiona muses.

A Warning.

In preparation for the trip, Fiona chooses to wear a bewitching grass-green silk gown with ribboned embroidery, discovered, by accident, in one of the large wooden wardrobe chest in the west tower. She takes the chosen gown to the seamstress to be pinned and altered to fit her to perfection. The sewing woman deftly takes a few nips here and little tucks there to make the gown quite suitable for the wearing.

Donning the dress the next day, Fiona is shocked and alarmed to find that all the seamstress's work has been undone, every pin, unpinned; every stitch, unstitched; every tuck, untucked. Pins were scattered haphazardly on the stone floor.

"Oh," exclaims Fiona, as she feels a chill saunter into the room. "The spirits are angry at me now, Why?"

The seamstress slyly says, "Perhaps you were not meant to wear this beautiful dress that once belonged to Lady Kyla. It was a special gift to her from Edmud."

"Give me strength!" though Fiona, with alarm.

She then recalls Una's warning, "Not one thing at the castle must change. When spirits visit, they must find everything the same as they had left it."

Much to her disappointment, there is no possible way that the lovely silk dress can be worn. Fiona must resort to wearing a simple, but pretty, garment from her own limited wardrobe.

"Spirits be damned. I will buy silks and satins... and sew my own gowns from now on," she vows, in a strong voice that is tipped with anger.

"On my return trip home from the Summer Progress at Lockmoor, I will shop at the market place for the loveliest materials I can find... like some shiny silks from the East, or some brocades from the continent. I have enough gold coins to dress like the Lady of the Castle Baine," Fiona happily thought.

Springs—and Fiona—have arrived in all their green glory.

CHAPTER FIFTEEN

The Sojourn.

Travel is slow. Fiona and her entourage follow a winding and convoluting route through the green and glistening hills, rounded and grass grown. Shepherds, in the distance, drive their flocks though narrow paths leading up the hillsides. The barking of alert Collies abruptly resound through the morning haze as these well-trained dogs keep the sheep together, driving back any headstrong sheep that would try to wander from the flock. One shrill mouth whistle from the shepherd alerts the dogs to the task at hand. It seems that all men of the Highlands, be it Lord or shepherd, need to be in control.

"Even the sheep seek greener pastures," muses Fiona, with an anxious laugh to herself.

Time passes, a snail's pace. The small caravan continues its crawl northward - criss-crossing the muddy roadways that lead to the Fair... bumping and jostling along on roads not shown on any map.

"These roads would be less muddy and cumbersome if the desperate peasants had not dug out most of the large rocks from the roadbed, stealing them away... to build their stone houses and huts," complains Fiona, with annoyance. Her inner thoughts falling on deaf ears!

Turning to the baby's nurse, she exclaims, "I am concerned about all the jousting baby Miah will have to endure before we reach the end of our sojourn."

"Not to worry, my Lady," responds the nurse, who now cradles the baby tenderly within her arms. Laughingly, she adds, "It seems the many ruts have rocked the precious little one to sleep, and dreamland."

The Fair.

Once they reach the Merkat Cross that marks the location of the Fair grounds, Fiona is suddenly filled with renewed anticipation—she has so loved the fairs of the past. She swears to herself that she must be part gypsy. The exotic smells and wonderful sounds light the senses with an electrifying jolt; the fair comes alive as the sweet aroma of jasmine from the east joins with the spicy smell of cinnamon from the west. The cacophony of sounds entraps her body, her being, silencing the winter's soundless noises of boredom and fatigue that have encompassed her life over the past few months. The hubbub and the gossiping crowds ignite her every bone.

"Ah, the wonderfulness of it all," Fiona sighs, as a childlike wonder comes over her being.

Meandering around the Fair grounds, amidst the throng, with Emil by her side, she glimpses Lord Avery, the handsomely dressed son of the pretentious and powerful nobleman, Jason Avery, who rules the land to the north of Castle Baine. The fine-looking man is considered the most "catchable catch" of all the young and rich available bachelors.

Eyes of gold meet eyes of green. Green, unlike the bottomless depths of all the oceans. Fiona, quite purposely, and with innocence, bumps into him. A fortuitous "bump" that only well bred women of the highlands know how to orchestrate. He helps her to her feet.

"My fair Lady, what a wonderful way to meet someone at the fair... and quite beautiful I might add."

At this, their first meeting, Fiona fauns shyness, and slightly bows during the introduction to the hale and hardy young gentleman, who, preening like a peacock, graciously takes Fiona's small hand in his, and brushes her fingertips against his cheek.

The man pontificates, "Fiona of Castle Baine, my pleasure, indeed." He manages a small laugh, albeit theatrical.

As quickly as this happenstance had taken place, young Avery moves off with an air of aloof indifference, engulfed in his own importance. As he turns away, he continues with his jovial jests and rakish comments to his traveling companions, a group of fun seeking young guards, regally outfitted in tunics that bear the regal crest of the griffin—the protectors of the lands of Avery Manor.

Fiona, suddenly, right then, right there, is sweetly smitten. Her libido quickens. Her heart races, quite like never before, like butterfly wing being caught in a flytrap. She is so enamored with this young gentleman's handsomeness and panache that she feels smothered, unable to breathe.

"Have I fallen in love at first sight?" she seriously questions herself.

"Good gods. Get me out of here, Emil," Fiona whispers breathlessly, "My heart is all aflutter."

"Beware of the man, Fiona. He is nothing but a ruthless rogue… just like his father," Emil snaps, his expression petulant.

"You'd be foolish to jump at dangled bait. For your own good, stick to your earlier proposed plan of action; rely on your own proven strategies. Do not lose your head… or your heart. You are playing with the devil," Emil warns.

He continues on. "I know the torrid tale of the dishonest Avery men… and their plundering… taking from others… taking from me… but that is another tale for another time."

"Tell me now," begs a flush-faced Fiona.

"Now is not the time. Look… the merchants await. You must make your purchases quickly so we can reach Lockmoor safely before dark," Emil orders tersely.

Safe Arrival at Lockmoor.

There was a sense of returning home, to a familiar beloved place. The ancient grove of trees still stands sentry over the fortress, heedless of time and the elements, casting deep shadows in the darkening twilight. Fiona's heart thumps wildly within her, almost matching the beat of the horses' hoofs as they pick up the pace, sensing the end of this long day's journey from Castle Baine.

"Home," sighed Fiona. "We are home… secure at last!"

From the group of servants and all and sundry assembled to welcome the arrival of the Lady of Castle Baine, Noah is the first to rush forward in greeting. In his haste, he all but tumbles into Fiona as she alights from the mud-splashed carriage. Laugher prevails as all witnessing the sight find this a welcomed venue of relief after the fearful and tedious journey across the countryside.

"Missy, excuse me and my unwarranted rush… but I was so concerned for your safety and the safeguard of our precious baby, Miah," Noah offered clumsily, his face turning crimson with embarrassment.

"Oh Noah, I, too, could not wait to see you and Una. We have so much to talk about and resolve. Please see to it that Miah and her Nanny are safe and sound inside. The baby was most restless during this day's trip. Surely the calmness of Lockmoor will quiet her whimpering."

After directing Emil and the servants with the task of unloading the goodly menagerie brought from Castle Baine and the wares and gifts bought at the Fair, Fiona joins Noah inside the Fortress.

In addition to the food supplies, Fiona has brought Noah a new leather whip, an ax, and a set of silver scarab knives. All of the gifts help to put a broad lighthearted smile on Noah's good-looking face.

"Ha, thinking of others again, Fiona? When will it be your turn to buy for Fiona?" Noah queries, with a wryly grin.

"My reason for these specific gifts has a double sided sword's edge. I hope you will teach me to use all three with perfection, should the need arise," responds

Fiona, as a dark shadow of concern moves across her face.

"This we can do. We will practice 'til you are as good as any man with these weapons. You already know some… I will teach you how to best use the scarab knife with its efficient six inch blade… so I will not have to worry about you so much," Noah states in dutiful speech.

"Thank you, Noah, for your help and your worries about me. But fret not. I also have plans that require that I make some extravagant purchases on the way home from this Summer Progress," continues Fiona, "but all that is in the future. First, I must speak to Una. My heart longs to sit down and talk with her."

"Una will be here at first light. She is aware of your arrival," replies Noah. "She concerns herself with regard to you. Prepare yourself, Missy, to hear good news and worrisome news as well."

The Much Awaited Sharing.

When Una arrives, she brings with her a burlap satchel brimming over with herbs, their flowering tips reaching in all directions as though blown by the wild north wind. As she set her bag down, sounds of tinkling music could be heard, indicating that Una had brought varied surprises with her, as well.

With a greeting of "Slainte," the two women rush to each others like lovers who have been separated for too long over time. Una cradles Fiona in her arms and strokes back her long brown hair that now hides Fiona's face and her quick tears of happiness.

Letting out a somber sigh, Fiona speaks in earnest, "Una. Thank the gods. I have missed you so."

"Not to worry, little mother. In these last few months, I know that you felt me near you. When you cried out on those dark and sobering nights, all I could do was listen. I lit the bailey candles and sent the smoke through the grayness of the night to Castle Baine, calling on the spirits to protect you. You are safe momentarily, but I come to ask you what has been threatening you within the last few days that brings the dark spirits to gather and cluster around you again?"

"The last few days?" queried Fiona, her face turning ashen. "It isn't baby Miah and her cough, is it?

"No. Not baby Miah. It is all about you. As I closed my eyes to sleep last night, I had a premonition that something was wrong. Clouds of hatred, something evil... as if someone or something is making plans to harm you, or rob you and put you to shame, surrounded you. Tell me exactly what has transpired during your trip here to Lockmoor," Una demanded.

"That is actually what I wanted to talk to you about, Una. At the Fair, I met young Lord Avery, and my heart was beating in my chest like a wild stallion trying to break out of his first harness. I felt weak all over... and told Emil so. He warned me that I was making a terrible mistake flirting with evil."

Fiona's voice trails off as she tries to digest the newly spoken warning. Were they, in any way, connected?

"Emil is a very smart man and possesses first and second sight. He understands the strange forces of the universe and the intricate web only spirits can weave. The warnings are an omen. Can one explain this connection? Let us see."

"We must again cast the rune stones against the wind for further clarification in this labyrinthine puzzle."

The Telling of the Rune.

Una rummages through her burlap bag and draws out the black stones of fate—the predictors of the future. She casts the dark stones upon the floor and the 24 runes roll and magically land face down. "Pick but one stone," she urges Fiona.

Fiona does as ordered. She chooses one stone showing a roughly imprinted character of the Viking alphabet; it looks like an "N" has been carved into its face.

Una goes on with her instructions: "Concentrate on the sign and let it come into your mind. Close your eyes tightly. Take a letting-go breath, and now another. Concentrate on the next out breath… and the next. On the next out breath, mentally concentrate on the sign on the face of the stone. Roll the stone over in your hands. Keep your eyes closed, and let the thoughts come into your mind. Tell me what you see, Fiona."

After a few moments of hesitation, Fiona murmurs, "I see the Avery manor. Smoky black clouds are rising from the chimneys. There is dark red blood seeping from under the large front gate. Wait…

I hear laughter, and I hear weeping at the same time. Two men… their hands are raised… they are pointing at me. Oh my god, this is an unnerving scene. Can this be true? What could the Averys have against me?" the nervous Fiona asks in a voice filled with woefulness.

"Tell me what to do to make this horrific sight go away!"

"The blood is a sign that your heart is in danger. Your heart is being used as a toy. I will make you a drink combined from the protective herbs of hawthorne and black cohosh so that your heart will never be tricked again, my dear Fiona."

"While you are here at Lockmoor, rest and fortify yourself. Grow strong. Your flagrant love for an evil Avery has sapped your strength, needlessly. It is time for you to overcome your helplessness and control your thoughts. No more travailing," Una sternly orders.

"I will try," responds Fiona, in a weak voice.

"Do… or do not," commands Una, "There is no try."

"You have been though so much Fiona, and you have learned how to keep the evil spirits in abeyance. You must not weaken now. Rebuild your strengths and your fortitude. Trust your intuition. Balance your cloudy head with solid roots. You can do it! You have come this far… you can go to the top of the mountain."

"If this is a game the Averys are playing, see to it that you are the player and not the pawn. Sharpen your weapons. Believe that you can be a wiser player than your enemies be."

"Come Fiona, the time is now to dissolve any darkness that surrounds your heart and to bring light to your thinking."

The Game of Hearts.

Raising her hands to the heavens, Una calls out, "Forces of the universe, come. Come Air, Fire, Water, and Earth. We need your power, oh mighty spirits, to fight the devil at the door."

"Come spirits of the trees, bring inner strength of mind and will, now."

"Come, spirit of the water, wash over Fiona like a waterfall and flow though her the way that a river flows through the sand at its bottom. Let the water cleanse all fear that surrounds her heart."

Placing her hands quite gently on Fiona's head, Una continues her ritual. "Tine choisricthe (sacred fire), come into Fiona's heart so she is blessed with wisdom, fortitude, and knowledge. Biodh se amhlaidh. So be it!"

This being done, Fiona's eyes flutter open, and she repeats, "So be it!"

As she rises to her feet, Una smiles at Fiona contentedly. "Come. Now you are ready to plan for justice. It is your turn now. Your turn to be in control of the elements. Time for evenness... a leveling of the dueling field. Time to bay at the man in the moon!"

At that precise moment, the susurrant wind stirs the tapestry in the window-- bringing with it love, hate, evil, and plans-- and the game of hearts begins.

CHAPTER SIXTEEN

The Game.

To activate their scheme of entrapment, Una and Fiona decide to duplicate a plan of Courtly Love—not too unlike the sophisticated cult of love and wild emotion that had spread hastily from the courts of France and readily copied by the elite of the Highlands... a practice of wooing and being wooed... valentines and Cupid's arrow... poems of romance written to tempt the emotional needs and sexual appetites of a woman.

The women make the decision, "Turnabout is fair play. It is time to tempt the needs of a man."

"Man's sexual appetite is stronger than a woman's," analyzes Una, with a sly, knowing grin.

"As a woman, you are capable of the great subtleties of a poet, are you not, Fiona? Write to your new love, young Jason Avery, tell him that he is the object of your worship; you suffer the torments of being his lover. Pretend you have fallen in love, madly in love... at first sight."

Fiona had to laugh at Una's wild plan.

"You have always guided me wisely, Una. I trust your thoughts in this matter," Fiona smiles. "I do believe I can conjure up some romantic words, indeed!"

Preparations are thus set in motion to seduce Lord Avery. He is to be sent a courtly note of unrequited love, words in rhyme that sing from the page, written in the passionate code of the troubadours. Fiona chooses an Ink of the iris root to be added to tease this man's senses with the sweet aroma of violets, to make his mind and body vulnerable, ripe for the taking.

"Yes, I will scribe something vague, something evocative, teasing... something that will set his evil heart thinking that I am truly obsessed with him. Young Jason Avery will rue the day he met me!"

Ah, where to begin in this cat and mouse game... a game of entrapment... of land ownership, pretension, lies, and evil deeds...and false promises!

Hot flashes behind her... her angst settling at last... Fiona is determined to be the lead player... to dominate... to take control! She rubs her small hands together, the left hand encircling the right, as each pointer finger points to the moon, to her destiny, oblivious to the skies of night.

Plans in Motion.

Emil is not without tasks. After seeing to Fiona's and baby Miah's settling-in at Lockmoor, he is charged with returning to Castle Baine to oversee the castle cleaning as all is set in perfect order, including the white washing of the stone walls of the Great Room after the grit and grime are scrubbed away, and the outdoor airing of the regal tapestries so they will blow clean in the soft summer wind. He must direct the planting of the fertile glens. Above all, he must guard the castle keep and its most precious possessions from scapegraces and scalawags... from thieves from without... and thieves from within... the living and the dead... the banshee and the burrows... whoever continue to seek revenge in the deep and deadly night.

Alas, these are many and mighty tasks, but Fiona recognizes Emil as a dependable man, one gaining in personal power and wisdom, for he has wisely learned how to coax vegetables from the rocky soil, and knows full well how to strike fear in the hearts of those under his command. His chores must be quickly and aptly accomplished in one month's time for he will then return to Lockmoor to guard Fiona and her troupe on their return trip back from Summer Progress.

On his way back to Castle Baine, Emil, the lone rider heading north, delivers the first letter to Avery Manor... because it is Fiona's wish that he do so. The letter is penned, "To Lord Avery."

Letter Received.

As fate would have it, the senior Avery, Jason Avery I, is the first to receive the letter and he is convinced that the sweet words are addressed to him, as he knows he is the more commanding figure of the two Averys. First he holds the letter to his aquiline nose and breathes in the redolent, sweet smelling fragrance of violets.

He reminisces, "Ah, the sweet smell of a woman..."

Intrigued, Jason rips open the envelope and reads the note written in a flourished hand. His heart begins to beat wildly in anticipation.

When first upon you my eyes did happen to gaze
My heart was wounded and magically ablaze
Like magic I loved you from the very start
Love aimed well when he shot his arrow deep into my
heart.
It is fate that we share love's destiny, do you agree?
Answer my quest, set my aching and anxious heart
free.
Signed this day by Fiona of Castle Baine.

The elder Jason throws his head back and roars in laughter. "Is this woman a fool?" he asks himself.

"So childish, so naive to think that I would ever be interested in her. Interested in her property, a definite yes. But then again, I understand she is a pretty sight. I do not know what her plans are.... Can I trust her motives?" Jason asks, his head spinning with possibilities.

"If she is interested in me, let her pursue this matter... and I will respond in kind. Two can play at this game. But for now, Fiona, I will just get on my high horse and wait."

Lord Avery muses on, amusing himself."Yes, Fiona of Castle Baine... you do present a most intriguing... and sensuous challenge."

A Warning.

Days pass and Fiona hears not a word, not hide, not hare, from the Avery manor and her apprehension mounts. Although annoyed and maddened, she decides to try one more time to entice her powerful, land hungry neighbors into her strategic plan of "let's pretend." A tangled web, indeed!

When it was time to send the second courtly letter, Fiona asks Noah to deliver it. Noah refuses adamantly, much to Fiona's surprise, as he has always submitted to her wishes in the past.

Noah is staunch in his refusal. "I will teach you your weapons of choice, Missy, but I will not participate in your recklessly tempting evil. Find someone else to do your foolish bidding."

"Before you take your game of wits too far, Missy, there is a worrisome sight that I must show you. Come with me now. Let us take a walk to the meadow," Noah commands.

As the two move toward the meadow, Fiona realizes that they are heading to the sight of Steward's final resting place. Her heart is in a panic. Nearing the grave, Fiona sees that the once dark dirt now is partially covered with brambles, yet there are signs of disruptive diggings. The stalwart gallan (standing stone) has been pushed from its solid sole sentry perch atop the grave, and now lies useless at the bottom of the death mound... protecting nothing!

"Gods, what has happened here? Tell me who did this!" The sight of the desecrated grave sent a sudden unexpected chill through her.

"This must be a warning from the gods," suggests Noah, putting his strong protective arms around the woman. Her body begins to tremble.

"In case someone is tampering with your thought and your will, I must move the heavy stone to where it can stand guard against evil once more," Noah says, in an effort to comfort Fiona.

Noah begins to reset the large stone.

"I hope that only Steward's good spirits have been privy to your latest plans to trick the Avery men out of their property. As for me, I do not think it is a good idea to sell your soul to gain land," Noah preaches in a condescending tone.

Standing tall, her determination coming alive, Fiona pushes Noah away. She waved a dismissing hand, "Nonsense," she said, her lips a grim straight line.

Stamping her foot on the ground, she adamantly continues. "I can do this! It is a good plan. This plan will right all the wrongs the Averys have done to you, to me, to Emil. Even Steward had suffered at the hands of these corrupt men as well. I know Steward will send his spirit of revenge to help us in our efforts to punish all the sinful misdeeds committed by the Averys... no injury, past or present, should ever be forgiven," says Fiona, with a look of religious resolve.

"It is not your place, Missy, to act as judge and jury. The three Fates spin and cut the thread of life-- every event predetermined. Do not arouse their ire by generating your own dangerous plans to do evil and tempt fate. How will your mindless shenanigans affect baby Miah? Think about that!"

His stinging words shrilly dart through her heart.

After a momentary silence, Fiona, gathering her fortitude, full force, responds.

"Do not be a fatalist, Noah. The world is evil, filled with wicked men... wicked deeds. I am determined to right the wrongs done to those I love… done to me! Justice be damned!"

Fiona moves closer to him and convincingly whispers, "We are doing the right thing. The spirits are on my side. And Noah, I know you will always be there to protect me."

Courting Love.

And so it is that Fiona must choose to send one of the other servants with the second note to the young Avery… much to her chagrin… and a personal disappointment in Noah who remained obdurate in his refusal to deliver her message. The script reads:

When night comes over, I awaken from my dreams
Of love-- Dreams that I have nightly
I see you in knightly armor, golden, shining brightly
You come to my bed that is rose-petal laden
And wrap me in rapture; my heart you do capture
As we bid all worldly cares adieu.
Your secret Love, "F".

As the second note is delivered to the front gate of Avery Manon, Jason Senior greedily retrieves it as his own. At the older age of fifty, such a game of love making, at its finest, could cheer his very soul, rejuvenate his very limbs, and perhaps reinstate his state of manliness. Not that he himself has been extremely lacking in sexual activity, or romping about, indecently indeed, as one of the maids at the manor is ever ready to try to satisfy his rash craving for fornication when the desire arises. Ha, the challenge of a new adventure… or a new love tryst… at his age, makes him chuckle with sheer yearning. He feels sexually stimulated.

Avery gathers all the old country love notes he had sequestered away in his wardrobe- letters stashed away in an aged black velvet pouch- lustful letters. He harbors the aroma- and ignores the brown edges. Does he have many? Of course he does. "Silly damsels in distress," he muses on.

He reviews and finds himself quite fond of the ones that began- "My love- I desire you…" and "From my breast- I mercy banish…" Before he responds to "F"- he looks over his other notations. He finds himself doting on the lines- "Kiss the fresh dew from your lips…" "Meet me between Venus and Mars…" and "If I were a knight, I'd be a slave to you…"

Lost in reverie, he quite thinks about women… so angry- weary- pining for lost loves- looking for new loves… with old husbands… wishing they had their lives to live over… desperately needing a roll over in the clover.

After reading… and rereading the fragrant note from Fiona, Jason reaches a decision; he commits to being a willing player in the game and readily, voluntarily, responds to the Lady's suggestive words. He is quite placated to copy words from an old note he had received from a past admirer; he remembers her pretty pretenses, but not her name. A face is a face.

"This could be the start of an adventure, a lucrative adventure, for me!" His silly mind now rolls around in verse. "Ha! Romance! Ants in pants." He chuckles to himself about his cunning cleverness as he begins to write.   He prints in large bold letters:

Judge me not harshly by the lateness of my response,
I do have a heartfelt desire to gaze upon your face
To hear your voice and have the angels sing
For your promising words set my heart fluttering
I will be your knight in shining armor
I will slay dragons on my way
Hoping you will gently to me say
Don't go- Stay
And if the flame of love exists at our first glance
You are the love mate I will gallantly romance.
Jason

This message is delivered to Fiona by one of Jason's guards, decked in the Avery crest of the golden griffin on his dark purple tunic. Fiona tells the guard to remain while she reads the response she has long awaited.

Jason, the admirable game player, follower of the rules of love as he so chooses, has elected to enclose, as well, a white lace handkerchief embroidered with the letter "A". The added note reads, " A gift of love… befitting my lady."

"So," Fiona pleasingly surmises, "the handsome scoundrel wants to play my game." She experiences a tingle of excitement. "But, me thinks he is too young a pup to be out alone, I am sure he has guidance from his father, who Emil said is the bigger scoundrel of the two Averys."

After reading his welcomed verse of agreeable pursuit, Fiona tells the guard to return to the manor, and to give Lord Avery a one-word message, "Continue."

The Responses.

Within the following weeks, Fiona receives two more love letters from Lord Avery. She shares both of these roughly romantic, implicative, demanding correspondences with Una, who scans the letters with a critical eye.

In the first note, Lord Avery tells of his professed desire to meet Fiona:

I will mount my winged steed and ride thru the heavens
Midst twinkling stars that sparkle like diamonds
That I will grasp from the sky without care
And gently braid them into your soft, silken hair.
I desire to kiss the fresh dew from your lips
To embrace you and feel the touch of your fingertips
If our hearts race wildly but can stand true
I will surrender and yield myself up to you. *Jason.*

Una's raised eyebrows show her trepidation at the reading of the last, short, cryptic message from Jason:

You anguish me with your promise of secret love
I need to kiss you on the mouth again and again-
And mark you as mine... so our love can prevail.

I will seek you at the castle where you abide
In your own eyes only the truth will tell the tale.
Jason

"I find Lord Avery's words very unsettling. He wants to meet you at Castle Baine. Why there? Stay true to your plan, Fiona, and never flee from his gaze or he will know you are out to deceive him, for he is a suspicious man."

Stillness enters the room; the two women stare at each other, a flicker of recognition of the dangers to come, lost in their own concerns of safety. Una speaks first.

"Your mind will be well prepared by the time you leave Lockmoor, so will your fighting skills... if you follow what Noah has aptly taught you. I will come to you in time of trouble, just send word of my need to be present, and I will be at your side. Till then, Emil will be your protector."

Putting her arms around Fiona, she adds, "You have made many positive changes over these past few weeks. I sense that the weighty black stone of death has been lifted from your heart."

"You now are stronger... and wiser. Continue to believe in yourself and all good things will come to you... only you can make your plans a success. But if you have learned nothing else over your time spent here, know this. When you fraternize with Jason Avery, a truly baneful man, you are dancing with the devil himself."

Una completes her warning, "Never trust him!"

"Remember, when your actions are scrupulous, none will question your motives. The first unguarded words that spill from your mouth could be your undoing."

"But there are measure you must take to prevent Jason Avery's wickedness from ever entering Castle Baine," instructs Una, handing Fiona three small jars of brightly colored incenses.

"Sprinkle the four corners of the Great Room with Angelica and Althea powder. This will ward off evil and aid your psychic powers of alertness. The third jar is Borage, carry it on your person at all times... it will strengthen your courage. You will not flinch from Jason Avery's gaze."

Foreboding.

But Fiona's thoughts are elsewhere—lost in the mystic air of uncertainness. Plans are now complete. She is to meet young Jason Avery again, face to face. Has she miscalculated the actions of this rascal?

It comes to pass that on her return trip to Castle Baine, Fiona plans a stopover at the Fair for necessary personal essential items needed to be in readiness for her intended meeting with Jason Avery. The list given her by Una is an arm's length long. Emil balks at this frivolous shopping spree, and tempers his temper by kicking at loose stones with the toe of his large boot, like a spoiled child in a tantrum.

Fiona simply responds, "Emil, I have needs too.... And many special items are imperative to this risky and dangerous game where winner takes all."

151

Fiona moves closer to Emil, and, standing on tiptoe, whispers softly into his ear, "And some of the purchases, I am sure, might surprise... and please you, as well!"

"Your whims are all well and good if the weather stays on your side. We will make our return to Castle Baine in the morn. But the breeze is beginning to build, it smells of earth and air and a mossy scent that means only one thing: a thunderstorm... or the forewarning of black clouds of danger."

CHAPTER SEVENTEEN

To her delight, just being at the Fair grounds infuses life into her mood and lifts Fiona's feelings. Thunderclouds have dispersed, leaving salmon clouds in their wake; the sun awakens. Her heart dances, liberated and free, like a bird on the wing... gliding through the misty sunlight.

"All is right with the world when I am in this place," admits Fiona's inner voice, both innocent and childlike.

Ah, and there is many a coin in my pocket to spend as I please.

The Encounter.

The merchants stalls are brightly decorated with banners that flutter in the cool breeze, and jammed with glorious items for sale or barter, depending on one's genius for trading or need for trinket or chattel. Around the food tents, the noisy crowd is pushing and shoving, creating the ever-existing sounds of laughter and life. Fiona is in her glory here at the Market Place; her spirits soar!

This sense of euphoria is soon to be shattered by a surprising and sudden encounter. While engrossed in purchasing yards of Eastern chatoyant silks from the Orient, and colorful satins from the West for her personal wardrobe, Fiona is suddenly startled by the resonance of a man's voice, deep, self important, and chillingly nearby.

"Perhaps these pale colors do not do you to perfection, my Lady. I believe the green silk would do the most justice to your sparkling eyes."

Fiona turns on her heels quickly, only to face a tall, somewhat husky, dark gray haired man. Her heartbeat quickens. Her pulse begins to race.

"Fiona, I presume. You are just as I have envisioned... quite lovely. Forgive me. Have I have acted too precipitously? Allow me introduce myself, my lady. I am Lord Avery, Jason Avery, your neighbor south of Castle Baine. We have met in words, loving words. An intercourse of verbiage!" He smilingly adds.

The words, *"We have met in loving words"* fly through Fiona's mind like large stones propelled from a catapult... at close range. Alarm flows over her. Frightening her. Then, like a silver bolt of lightening, she realizes her blunder. Her heart ices over with cold fear. Her brain turns stormy...

Oh no! Spare me! It is the old man! I have not trapped the younger Avery in my snare as I had hoped. No! I have trapped the elder Jason Avery, the better and more vicious player of the two men... the prized opponent!

"It is my pleasure to meet you before our planned encounter, one week hence," the man continues, a strange smirk upon his moist lips.

"Thank you," Fiona responds in a shilly shally and quite irresolute manner. She has just lost her first moment of control.Gathering her wits about her, Fiona points to the colorful bolts of fabric on display. She blurts out, "I will choose green. Your wish is my command, Lord Avery."

She turns slightly so as not to reveal the rosy color of embarrassment that has flooded her cheeks.

The elder Jason Avery is taken aback by the shyness of this woman.

"You seem somewhat bewildered, Lady Baine. Were you expecting someone else? Someone younger, perhaps?"

"No! No! You are just fine… just the handsome man I pictured you to be," Fiona lies expertly, looking directly into Jason's eyes. Her composure returns full force.

"It is good that we are both pleased."

Jason takes her trembling hand in his and raising it to his lips, brushes her graceful fingertips with a kiss.

"Till our meeting then, Fiona." Jason adds before he strolls away. The image of this vivacious vixen imprinted in his mind returns a smile to his thin lips.

So, my dear Fiona, are you ready for my game of love and hate? You are a most lovely and welcomed challenger.

Exiting the Fair grounds, bold loving words bolt through Lord Avery's mind. He laughs to himself as he readily composes his next courtly letter to the charming, rich Fiona, Lady of Castle Baine. Mostly, he is bemused by his own wit with words, his ability to make words rhyme, "face… grace"… as he mentally composes his note to his pretty new prey.

**I am obsessed with your sensuous gifts of beauty
and grace
Since our fortuitous meeting you torture my mind
with lust
I am yearning to bed you down and kiss your face
Do complete these dreams that pain my heart, oh
so much.**

The Big Game.

When Jason's note, a monologue of love, is
delivered, read and absorbed, Fiona knows full well
that the big game has begun, with the stakes anted up.
Spurred on to complete her new schemes and reset her
traps with renewed confidence and vigor, she muses:

*I have less then five days to be ready, but with
the help of the castle servants... and the spirits, the
good and the vindictive, I will carry out the plans made
at Lockmoor... with some major changes meant for the
elder Lord Avery.*

*First, the seamstress must create my special
dress of green satin. And, most critical, I will intensify
the aphrodisiacs to assure Jason's lust for love be
sufficiently aroused and satisfied.*

"Yes. You will get your green gown... my dear
Jason... and a little more than you bargained for."

Readying For Entrapment.

The original plan set by Una and Fiona at
Lockmoor was a simple one--appealing to the sensual

desires of the younger Avery, known for his sexual prowess and seductive ways with women. It would only take a few bites of the forbidden fruit to turn the young man's interest to lustfulness, but now the game has changed with the appearance of a new player—a more practiced player.

Arrangements change from simple to complex. Emil must oversee the selection of more... many more... specific items for the affaire d'amour between Fiona and the roguish older Jason.

So he sets to work directing the household in the tasks at hand. Marigolds and lavender flowers, favored for their mesmerizing fragrances, must be cut from the castle garden; golden honey gathered from the beehives, juicy fruit picked from the boughs of the apple trees growing wild in the orchard, tasty pine nuts gathered from the deeper woods, and ripe onions and garlic dug from the kitchen garden.

Finally, Emil orders the succulently sweet dates and figs bought at the fair be examined for crawling creatures, great and small, and readied for consumption... all in accordance with Fiona's new wishes. He knows full well these foods have been chosen not only for their taste and aromas, but also for their power to ignite the aging libido.

Master Avery will be so bombarded with a lustful fire from within his loins that he will act on Fiona's every whimsical move," chides Emil to himself.

But there is more to this plan than even Emil knows. According to Gaelic superstition and magic, the use of succulents as aphrodisiacs for knaves of the kingdom brings about the male's preoccupancy with sexual gratification to such a degree, that he will be unmindful of the logical thoughts that run through his brain and oblivious of the spirit forces that surround him… exposing his weaknesses.

And so it is that Fiona's use of arousing foods and scents will dim the keenness of Jason's mind, halting his shrewdness, rendering him totally ignorant of the forces of air, wind, and fire, and the spirits of the Vibes who surround Fiona, protecting her… their chosen one.

CHAPTER EIGHTEEN

The Feast Begins.

A thick white mist rises and blankets the glens on the morning of the scheduled liaison between Jason and Fiona. Above, Fife birds soar and swoop, freely, aimlessly, in the blue and cloudless sky. The towers of Castle Baine appear through the mist, through the shroud of reality. The tops of the tallest trees look like islands in a blue sea where the white gulls dip for sustenance.

As he nears his destination, Jason is caught up by the beauty of it all, a sign of welcome to behold... the castle of his dreams.

In his reverie, Jason had never imagined the magnitude of Castle Baine. The great towers, seventy feet high, boasts of battlements and a wall walk for its guardians—the soldiers. From this position, the men-at-arms could see cross-country for miles. The towers, freshly whitewashed, glistened in the dazzling sun of midday. A bright red and gold banner flutters in the breeze from its highest point. Both beautiful and foreboding. This massive stone icon, surrounded by huge stonewalled courtyards, warned all to beware—"Touch me not!"

Upon arrival, Jason and one of his senior guards from Avery manor, donned in a tunic festooned with the crest of the invading griffin on a field of purple, the color symbol of the equestrian, commandeer their horses forward. Finding the great iron gate of the first tower already open wide to allow entrance, the two horsemen quickly gallop across the wooden drawbridge, then under the raised portcullis, and onto the grounds of Baine Castle.

I must find a way to make this great castle mine... all mine!

There is the deafening abrasive sound of the iron gate that, as it is lowered, plummets downward with the thunderous thud of a guillotine. A decisive crash! He could feel the vibration in his chest. It shocks him back to reality... and spurs a dark apprehensive feeling... *Has my escape been cut off as well?*

His path takes him to the castle's second courtyard where the horses are corralled. They are magnificent steeds—from great war horses that could carry a heavily armored knight into battle, to Coach Horses that pull the plows, to saddle horses— from the Clydesdales of Scotland to the Hackneys and Thoroughbreds of England, all displaying wide girth and legs that can illicit power on command. "Seventeen to eighteen hand high" Avery quickly observes.

One steed is being shod by the farrier (blacksmith) as Jason passes. He smells the molten iron, and thinks, "I will ride you one day, and put my spurs to your hind side, and make you race against the wind of the highlands!"

"I will actually stick some cotton up your nose to allow you to breathe less, and force you to run faster." A trick he learned as a boy.

Can I learn more? —Avery muses as he goes through the third courtyard. It is vast!

Here he finds a dozen, or so, of the men of the garrison actively practicing their skills in arm-to-arm combat with wooden swords. A knight on horseback tilts at a shield mounted with a counterbalance with his tip-covered lance. Hawks in cages line the far stonewall. These birds, still wearing their jesses or leather thongs attached to their legs and soft leather hoods, are being readied by the attendants for falconry--hunting with a falcon or hawk. The bird will fly from the attendants' wrist, snatch its unsuspecting prey, and bring it to earth.

"It seems your defenses are ever ready, Fiona. But who is your prey? Are you the falcontress of this castle? Can I find protection within these walls? I need answers before the need arises," he thinks meditatively.

"Let us move on," Sir Avery says to his accompanying steward. He shakes his head slowly in disbelief, totally unprepared for the myriad of emotions that quite engulf him in surprise… and confusion.

The fourth courtyard portrays the everyday life of a castle in its mundaneness. The women are making wine. Grapes have been gathered into hug whicker baskets from the orchard. The aroma assails him. Luscious grapes coupled with apples and pears. So fragrant! So sweet smelling! White sheets, pinned on clotheslines, flap about in the billowing wind, and the wind quite eradicates stains of both lords and ladies, left on linen. Very fine linen. Imported linen.

He wonders not where the washwomen and chambermaids sleep. They can always be found in the second floor of the tower. Rolled in a blanket—

keeping warm—keeping warm by the heat of the fire of the great hall that ekes its way slowly… and frugally… through the wooden beams beneath them as they sleep on the wooden floor.

"I will make time to bed each and every one of them," Jason muses, with an evil hollow laugh.

His sardonic thoughts vanish the moment Fiona appears in the doorway. A vision. She stepped into the courtyard, the picture of confidence. Outfitted in a lovely forest green satin gown, as promised… jolting him back to reality.

Her garment has been deftly copied from one the regal gowns that hang in Kyla's wardrobe.

I have torn a page from your book on how to dress like a lady, dear Lady Kyla mused Fiona, somewhat caustically.

She moves toward him with careless elegance. Jason appraises her appearance with the trained eye of a critic. The fitted bodice of Fiona's gown is styled to reveal her small but adequate young breasts; its flowing green full skirt, nipped and tucked at her thin waist, suggests a hint of white under gown with each tiny step she takes. She wears no headdress, but her Lady in Waiting has tied gold and silver ribbons, that simmer in the sunlight, in her long silky brown hair. She wears no jewelry nor adornment; instead she has chosen to deftly wind a second amulet, a bracelet made of senna, mint, and rue, around her slim wrist… a double aegis to twice shield her against all evil transgressions.

Jason is pleased beyond words and feasts his eyes on this pleasing delicacy of womanhood standing before him, and gives a wink of an eye to his dismounting companion.

This evening should be most intriguing... and perhaps more.

Taking her small hand in his, he raises it to his lips and professes his pleasure with a kiss. "Slainte' Fiona."

Fiona, too, finds herself unexpectedly satisfied with the semblance of her former adversary, Jason, the man she continues to reevaluates through lowered lashes as she acts the part of the demure Lady of the castle... and surprisingly, she likes what she sees... a man, husky, yet tall... a dark, yet friendly quality about him which makes him appear sensual... and almost desirable.

His gentleman's black weskit is tied around his somewhat large waist, giving him the look of one who has partaken of much liquid libation over his lifetime. He sports a distinguished silver gray beard; his long black hair is streaked with gray. But alas, it is his dark, almost black eyes, which give him a most handsome look.

Are these splendid eyes revealing him to be a rogue? Why had not Emil told me more about the sexuality of this man? A facade? Perhaps-- But his remarkable good looks will make my task of seduction most interesting.

Her skin actually tingles with anticipation as the thoughts of tonight's "game" flash in her mind. Fiona has prepared well for the evilness, coupled with charm, of this man... *so bring it on!*

The Evening Progresses.

Capricious thoughts tumble through Jason's mind; he allows them to settle in quietly. They turn into wanton desires of possession... seduction... and simple, raw, gratification.

Jason fantasizes. *Fiona has far more beauty and style than I had expected to find in a young woman. She is so agreeable to my words and actions that it should be easy to make my written promises of love and desire come true. After we feast on the culinary delights, I will feast on her with delight. I will lead this young, eager widow, who has been long lacking in sexual satisfaction, no doubt, to her very own bedchamber for a taste of experienced manhood.*

Ah, but first a little wine is needed to numb her somewhat rigid controls... drinking has always relaxed my conquests of the past... and loosened their tongues. Ha, Fiona, are you clever enough to play the game?

The Players Continue.

Entering the great hall, Jason is aware of the hustle and bustle going on around him; much is being done to make his supper one that is meant for an honored guest. And he does feel special. The servants have poured the red, red wine that Jason greedily gulps down before he realizes that he had planned to propose a toast to the Lady of the castle.

He refills his goblet, holds it high, and stammers on.

"To Fiona of Castle Baine, I come in good faith. I raise my cup in friendship, admiration, and peace. May our paths truly unite as one in destiny."

"To us," says Fiona, with a fleeting half smile.

Fiona, absorbed with her own devilish plan, to bare Jason's primal emotions through food and wine, much wine... too much wine... bemusingly adds a toast to herself, *"And may the spirits of Castle Baine be wise to your comings and goings, your evil ways and empty promises."*

The large oaken table of the Great Hall is spread with wonderful delicacies. The servants busy themselves with the elaborate presentation of the first course, appetizers of bilberry leaves and cohosh with picked eel, rich golden honey bread, and crushed pine nuts, all three renowned for activating the sexual appetite... a culinary love potion.

The second course is the eating of haggis, made from the entrails of the highland sheep, a purposeful delicacy said to quickly arouse a man's raw animal instincts. The main course, mutton, was chosen from the hillside herd, and fresh trout fished from the river Knell. The figs and dates, basted and candied in mead, sweet and succulent, complete the idyllic love feast.

Fiona, once pleased with the labors of the kitchen staff, shows displeasure with their constant idle gossiping and whispering. She beckons Emil to her side and chastises him.

"You must keep the servants in order. Do not let them spoil our game with their foolish chatter and tattling."

Emil responds, "Worry not about the servants, Fiona. I will deal with them handily. Stay centered on our plan."

Coincidences.

Jason now makes no sense at all. Satiated with animal entrails, mutton, and candied figs that he freely gorged at will—all these delicacies, plus the musky smell of a woman, have assaulted his maleness, and said body parts—transforming them into iron. He felt the need to meander around the great room... but feared such said parts would make a loud "clanking" noise as he pranced.

A gray film slitters across his eyes in unison with the gray film that now slides across the skies—obscuring the sun and dimming views of the far away cliffs and forest. The highlands he controls slip quietly from sight. No longer in focus. He finds himself quite alerted to the present by Fiona's presence and voice and lust. Lust—sensuous desire— hot bodily appetite—passion—joy! Innate sensual desire. And lust for her he does!

He reaches out with an unsteady hand for his wine goblet, spilling most of its contents down the front of his spotted weskit. It seems the older he gets, the more quickly he yields to alcohol's ability to spark his feelings of euphoria.

Just watching her firm and white breasts rise and fall with each breath invokes a familiar warm feeling in his loins. Sweat begins to form across his dark brows and trickles down toward his graying temples. His somewhat handsome face glistens in the glow of the gleaming candlelight.

What is happening to my control? I must not loose command of my body. I am here to discover the hidden secrets of Castle Baine. I must hear of her land and her treasures. Tell me all, Fiona.

The Questioning.

Jason's efforts to have Fiona share secrets proved to be a fool's errand. When he asks her about the former lords of the castle, Steward and Edmud, Fiona simply responds, "They both live in the silence of death, and have taken their secrets to the grave."

Not to be dismissed, Jason continues questioning. "What of your property? I have the need to view your land in the first light of day." The small twisted grin that appears across his mouth suggests shrewdness, but he slowly regains his posture of geniality.

"I am only suggesting that as neighbors, we should ride along our borders and agree on mutual protection. I need to see the land from the Castle Baine side of our common border."

"All in good time," responds Fiona, with a casual wave of her hand.

"For the moment, let us put our thoughts of property behind us and just let us enjoy what we see before us. Come now, Jason, a little more liquid libation... and I promise you this, before the evening is over, we will each share one secret between Castle Baine and Avery Manor."

Sharing of Secrets.

Drink they do... and Jason words become more and more that of a loosened tongued fool. He has never been so reckless. He is in love, smitten, feeling amorous and desirable of this beautiful lady. The fragrance of her ambrosia invades his nostrils and inner being, making him "woozy." All he can do now is hope he can have the opportunity to taste of her... to sample her body.

Perhaps it will be a matter of simple seduction... as she is but a simple woman... with simple thoughts and needs. She could be nothing more.

Fiona's words bring him back from reverie to reality! "Let me go first in the sharing of a secret. Play a little game with me! I will tell you the best secret of all-- the treasure of Castle Baine."

Instantly, a gleam flashes in Jason's eyes... a sobering gleam. He moves closer, not wanting to miss a word. He eases his strong arm around Fiona's delicate shoulder, a pleading gesture that urges her to continue.

"Let us begin this way. As tales of fairies and leprechauns that hid 'neath wild mushrooms of the highland forest – I will do the same." And Fiona begins.

"Once upon a time, the great and valuable golden coin of Augustalis was brought to this castle. I know of its hiding place."

"I, too, have observed that the younger son and merchant, Edmud, brought many great treasures from the grand European markets to Castle Baine. But I know nothing of a valuable coin!"

He pauses, "So, what does one have to do to learn the secrets of the golden coin?" the wide-eyed Jason asks, clearly expecting to be told the answer to the riddle.

"I will share that information with only my husband," Fiona adamantly replies, noting Jason's overwhelming curiosity about the coin.

The bait, clearly set, is now being nibbled on.

Her comment registers. Jason tries to clear his blurred mind, which now spirals out of control upon hearing the word, "husband."

A minute passes by, perhaps three. With eyes growing narrow and brows knitting together in deep concentration, Jason selects his one secret to share.

"Once I was a brave and bold knight. Fighting for the king, I amassed a small fortune of my own. Clever and brilliant fighting brought me awards of vast land, coins, castles, albeit at the mortal expense of insipid people. But insipid people have a need to die. Rot beneath the ground."

"But that is no secret, Jason."

"My secret is that I am willing to share my land with you, my lovely Fiona. If your heart is true, and you bear me a legitimate child... you and the child could inherit my lands, my great estate. What is mine could be yours."

With a sense of thrill escalating in her voice, Fiona inquires, "What of your son? Your son Avery, is it? He is quite as handsome as you, Sir Avery, I am told. A bit too bold and daring, perhaps?"

"I, too, will share that answer upon marriage," responds Jason, his voice somewhat unsteady.

Marriage! After a moment of stunned silence, Fiona reaches to the table to pour a silver goblet of wine. Raising it high, she proclaims, "We are in accord. Upon marriage then, the answer to our secrets will be shared equally as husband and wife. So be it, Birodh Se."

Jason listens, with body erect, or at least some vital parts of it are. Though his mind is cloudy, he knows full well that he can't let this opportunity slip through his greedy fingers... opportunity only knocks once! The promises of gaining acres and acres of fertile land, more power, and unknown riches, to boot... the life he must possess... are within his grasp.

His lust for Fiona deepens with each moment that passes. His eminent desire is to copulate this union, right now, right here, perhaps right on this table— pinning her against the oak wood and taking her—midst the spoils of a well-planned supper.

"Done!" says Jason, slamming his hand down hard on the table in agreement. Willing beyond words, Jason toasts to their accordance. "So be it."

My dear Fiona, when you play games, never ask a better player to play. I have won this game. Winner takes all.

By this time, the roving troubadours, situated in the quiet corners of the great room, with fingers raw from strumming, exit—in search of wages. They are quite aware that Fiona has picked up the imaginary gauntlet that Sir Avery has thrown down on the dusty floor.

"I wager that he will nibble on her apples tonight."

"And spit out the seeds," the challenged man of song retorts.

In the fading light, the River Knell has lost its sheen—turning black and fathomless. Darkness was coming fast—and with it—the chill of the autumn night settles in the highlands. And with it, its devilish ways.

A chill—a chill that embarrasses—evil, lost dreams and lost songs sung— promises to keep and secrets to be shared—but will the players in the game answer the call of the wind, honestly or dishonestly? No matter. The air will be cool with sadness at first light— chilling to the bone.

CHAPTER NINETEEN

Preparations.

Jason is ecstatic as he assumes the power over making the "wedding arrangements"… rather "business arrangements," which is more in line with his way of thinking. He has always been in charge and in control. This wedding is no exception. His every demand will be followed to the letter.

Snapping a peremptory command to his guard, Jason sends him in search of a man of the cloth to perform the wedding ceremony as soon as possible, hopefully within a week's time.

"Have the cleric here by the rising of the full moon."

A crisp breeze is just starting to blow from the lowlands as Fiona tends to her very own intricate plans. She will have Una travel up the River Knell to direct the final preparations in the rouse with the senior Jason Avery. It is a good wind. It will help assure Una's appearance at Castle Baine well before the guard can persuade a cleric of the church to leave the warmth of the friary.

"Jason can have his way with many of his wedding declarations- the music he wishes to dance to, the amusing jester and juggler who will entertain, the few guests he will welcome.

"It is best that I acquiesce to his controlling wishes," Fiona muses.

"With the help of Una and Emil, and the spirits... I will keep him off guard to that which I am about."

When Una arrives, she must formulate plans of action quickly in order to secure the aid of the spirits of Castle Baine. She implores the help of Kyla's spirit force by selecting the woman's favorite ornate hyacinth necklace for Fiona to wear as her wedding jewelry. The wearing of this gleaming stone by another woman will awaken the spirit's anger, and will handedly boost Jason's profound level of greed just by his thinking that such a treasure belongs to his young bride-to-be... and these gems will soon be his.

To keep the spirit's ire guaranteed, the seamstress is told to alter Kyla's red brocade ball gown so it will fit Fiona's slim body. The seamstress cringes.

"Please, m'lady, that beautiful gown was brought from Europe by Edmud, for the lady of the house, and for her alone. It should not be made into a wedding dress... or be worn by a younger woman. You will bring the wrath of the evil spirits down upon us!"

That is the intention... Red is for passion, anger, and blood, let's evoke Kyla's passion now. Kyla's spirit forces and strengths are needed in this place to defend this castle, thought Una.

Una orders the wedding meal, one that is heavy on the wine and light on the food... something an older man desires. There will be a first course of haggis, a main course of lamb baked in pine nuts and honey, and finally, stewed wild fruits especially picked from the orchard, to be laced with Una's special love promoting garnishes.

And lastly, the vital task is to prepare Fiona's mind for what is about to take place on the morrow, the wedding day. For this, Fiona is sequestered away to the upstairs bedchamber. Una prepares for the ritual with the laying of cloch stones in the shape of a six-pointed star in the fireplace. She places branches of green pine to follow the lines of the star and complete the symmetrical design. At each vertex of the six points, dried apple blossoms are added. The hearth's tinder is lit and flickers and glows brightly. Momentarily, a brilliant white flame bursts outward, illuminating the room with pointed shadows that dance and leap across the far wall, like pinnacles in orchestration to the flames' roar.

The ritual begins. Standing in front of the fire, the two women, with arms outstretched, share a chant to implore the gods' help in this time of great need.

Una prays in a low monotone voice, "Spirits of love and erotica enter this room. Spirits of air, wind, and fire, make this woman a temptation that cannot be resisted. Spirit of the Vates, make this woman a temptation that cannot be fooled."

Her voice rises now to a higher pitch. "Spirit of the Druids, make this woman a temptation that is protected by the positive and good karma of the dead."

Una concludes her spiritual pleas with the words, "Come spirits, all. Join our circle in this our time of need. Amen."

Onto the flame, ground acorns are scattered — acorns—from the mighty oak— honored by the Druids as the sacred Tree of Life—for its yawning roots penetrate as deep into the Underworld as its branches soar to the sky.

At first, little bright golden sparks wildly caper and crackle across the orange flame. Then, ominous bile colored smoke whooshes from the hearth, and billowing yellow smoke invades the room.

Una's black eyes darken with concern as she looks at Fiona, who flinches and sets her body into a frightening, upright position. She feels compassion for her long-standing friend.

"What does this mean? Is it a bad omen?" Fiona questions, perplexed. Her confusion turns to bewilderment. Sadness is the only message her eyes can convey!

"Be not afraid, Fiona. All is well. The "daur" has done its work. We have entry into the Other World itself. The gods have opened our minds to greater wisdom. They forewarn that we are trying to control evil. Jason is sinister… not a man to be fooled. But the gods will protect you as they promised."

"Please Fiona, kneel down, close your eyes and take two letting go breaths."

Laying her warm hand on Fiona's head, Una quietly whispers, "Center your thoughts on the gates of the spirit world."

"I call out to the spirits of Stewart, Kyla, and Edmund. Oh! Spirits of this castle, come forward to Fiona's aid if she calls out in the night. Let your power wash over her. Be her strong force against the evil of Jason… who schemes to take this castle from her …from you. Guard her through her wedding night and all the nights that follow. Keep her secure and out of harm's way. So be it, Biodh se amhlaidh."

"Biodh se amhlaidh," repeats Fiona, quite relieved to know that the ghosts of Castle Baine will be readily at her beckoned call, no matter where, no matter when.

For safety sake, I must keep my longest dagger beneath my bed pillow in order to shield me from the unexpected... thanks to Noah's training... I can wield this weapon with agility, Fiona reminds herself.

CHAPTER TWENTY

The Ceremony.

The startling sounds of a horn from the battlements of the keep, gleefully, cheerfully, announce the arrival of the wedding day. At Castle Baine, the wedding ceremony, simple, tasteful, is about to begin.

The couple to be wed makes for an interesting sight, unique, the bride-to-be... young and lovely... the groom, Jason, elderly and stoic. Fiona, is gowned in red, a brilliant red. Scarlet. Jason is surprised, as he had orchestrated the wedding scene in his mind to be more of his liking: a bride in white, virginal, receptive. Jason is dressed in black, both somber and serious, and well intended... to a certain degree.

Standing before the pair is the recently found cleric, a man of the cloth. A priest. He wears a shoddy brown wool robe; his hair is fashioned in a bluntly cut— tonsure style, thus revealing a very round baldhead, encircled by sparse wisps of dark hair. His plumb body is noticeably far from underfed. He tugs nervously at the cord encircling his oversized girth as if trying to set it free. A large golden cross, swinging to and fro around his fat neck, beckons peace to enter the room.

His appearance is definitely the hallmark of a Friar... according to Fiona's way of thinking.

The fat fingers of the cleric fumbled uneasily with the yellowed and frayed ribbons of his prayer book, seemingly anxious to start the ceremony. Next, to the astonishment of all, the lowly priest bends forward to kiss his amice—and is quite transformed into a man of the church—as he places it around his neck.

The monk crosses himself in blessing, using three fingers to represent the Trinity, dotting his forehead, stomach, right shoulder, and left. The wedding service begins at last.

"We have come together in joy to witness the marriage of Fiona and Jason," he says in a small voice. He then questions, "Is there anyone present who knows why this man and this woman should not be wed? Speak now."

The inquiry is directed to those congregated, a handful of servants in attendance, and hastily assembled guests invited by Jason, some earthy sheepherders, and several wealthier vassals who rent and tend the land. All position themselves in the spacious Great Hall of Castle Baine. Noticeably absent from the ceremony's guests is the younger Lord Avery.

Hearing the silent response to his query, the monk continues. "Well then, let us proceed with the liturgy."

The brief ceremony has three parts. First, the cleric places his thumb on the foreheads of both bride and groom and proceeds to traces the sign of the cross with holy water and oil—the sign of cleanliness and limpidness.

A short reading from the prayer book follows, according to the Ephesians: "Let wives be subject to their husbands because a husband is head of the wife... Paying honor to the woman as the weaker vessel... Husbands cleave to your wife. She hath risen in the night, and given prey to her household... Searching for peace... an empty gong."

Lastly, the wedding ring is blessed... the golden wedding ring, the Celtic Ring, a complete circle of the Claddagh... to be worn on the third finger of Fiona's left hand because, as those of a superstitious nature believed, that is the finger connected directly to the woman's heart... and she will obey, commit to the wishes of... her husband—the dominant male.

As the brief ceremony concludes, Jason and Fiona kneel in unison to receive the church's blessing over their marriage. From a common cup of blessed wine, the couple, denoting the sharing of joys and sorrow in the future, takes small sips. They are, in this act, called upon to "bear one another's burdens."

At this moment, Jason looks intently at Fiona. Their eyes meet. Fiona returns his steady gaze with an intently, honest stare. A small smile creeps across Jason's lips. He seems obviously pleased with her truthfulness. He believes in her.

The monk eradicates the lip marks of both bride and groom from the wedding chalice with a quick swipe of pure white linen. He now finalizes the service with the Latin words, "Dominus vobiscum."

Jason responds, Et cum spiritu-tuo—and with your spirit."

"Until death do you part. May this marriage be a source of moral strength and divine guidance, to which you need to be faithful to each other, and to rear your children in the love of God. Amen."

Looking at the mixed slap-up, and shoddy assembly, he gathers them in, declaring: "Blessed be the new life of this couple. Amen. So be it."

By contrast, the longer ceremony is the signing of legal papers that record the deeds of the great properties of Avery Manor and Castle Baine, binding them together on this day. The miles and miles of land are combined and willed to the surviving spouse, and/or their heirs, should either Fiona or Jason meet with the fate of death.

As the recording of signatures of both bride and groom on the two contracts completes his final legal act, the cleric quickly moves on to the banquet table and helps himself to the ale flavored bread and gravy trenchers filled to the brim with roast lamb. He eats like a glutton. He takes the wine into his mouth like an epicure of fine drink. The nectar of the gods drizzles from the corners of his mouth.

He then signals that his consumption of food and wine has ended by wiping his greasy hands on the front of his robe. He speaks quickly to his flock, the shepherd and the tillers of the field—the invited guests. "Peace be with you," he repeats over and over again to these followers of the church.

Having been paid, quite to his satisfaction, for his services in more than a fair amount of golden coins, the cleric departs Castle Baine, legal papers in hand, and coins jingling, jangling in the pocket of his robe. The rotund man of the cloth, albeit, scratchy brown wool, was quite gleeful as he departed the castle and its barrier walls. The rosary that hangs from his corded belt, its beads, large, wooden and round, swing in cadenced to the motion of each faltering step taken in his dusty leather sandals.

He heads back to his monastery in much better spirits than when he arrived. He is now full, content, and richly rewarded for his services... and he will readily spread the gossip, the tittle-tattle, of the wedding to the many travelers he will encounter along his route back to the friary.

Achievement.

The blood rushes to Jason's head as he contently thinks about his clever manipulations. This state of divine euphoria for the masterful deed he has so masterfully achieved, is welcome, indeed.

Castle Baine is mine at last... and I will soon have all its hidden treasures as well.

Fiona feels blissful now that she has completed Act I of her plan to control the three largest pieces of property – spreading from Lockmoor clear across the highlands, through Avery Manor, and on to Castle Baine.

My marriage to Jason has made this estate ownership possible... a great catch indeed it is. I must keep my wits about me in this game of survival... In winning, I can have all the land and its treasures for myself. Owning the land—the land—that is what is vital to survival. Survival—the cause. The reason for existence. Mine—and Miah's. Together we shall rule the property. The grand and glorious ownership—the power to be in control.

Control—the answer.

A Taste of Love.

His head whirls, dizzy with power, as it takes little drinking of the spicy mulled wine to put Jason in an erotic mood, ready to conquer Fiona, his young, rich, very rich, and sweet beautiful bride. Jason knows well that wine will nourish his body... open his arteries... and help in procreation... something to look forward to, indeed.

Having his fill of food and feasting, the bride and groom choose to dance to a romantic tune played on the musician's mandolin... a song of the highlands... a song of the oak groves... a song of sun lit shining rivers... and the land. Jason, surprisingly light on his feet, moves and twirls, turning about the Great Hall until his head is spinning; his libido, pulsating; his loins, on fire.

The celebration turns wild and frisky, wine flows, fiddles screech, guests become noisy. Happy dancers gaily twirl to the lively music of the reels and jigs, amongst the rose petals that waltz in bright array beneath their toe tapping feet.

Highlanders need no reason to dance, but a wedding will do!

Anxiety.

After dancing a round or two with Fiona, Jason anxiously awaits their tryst in the hay... *ah, the first of many...* for he assumes that as Fiona's body fits so softly... warmly... and quite perfectly... into his arms, she will be ever so more irresistible in the bedchamber.

As for Fiona, she acquiesces slowly to the thought of consummating the marriage. *I must not be caught pretending.*

What has happened to me?   Perhaps I have had one too many of the spiced apples... laced with the desire for love.

To Bed, to Dream.

In the shank of the evening, a white haired servant, holding his candle high, shuffles along the darkened passageway of the castle tower that leads both bride and groom to the master bedchamber especially prepared for the newlyweds.

Entering the room, Jason and Fiona are set at ease by the warming glow of the wood fire, just stoked in the fireplace. A mass of red scented candles, emitting the aroma of spicy cinnamon and mulberry, has also been lit, and their fragrance encompasses the room. As the old servant leaves, he hangs a single red rose on the outside of the door, alerting all that the bride and groom need privacy and are not to be disturbed 'til morn.

Jason slowly directs Fiona to the large straw bed in the center of the room... deftly, with panache... and style. A vital, sobering thought comes to his mind: he must discover the secrets of Castle Baine as he was promised. Thus, he must deny his body's cravings for wanton satisfaction for a few moments more.

The Sharing of Secrets.

"Before I make you truly feel like a woman, let us share the answers to our secrets proposed a few days ago," Jason says in a pedantic tone.

Jason takes a moment to caress her within his arms and softly kisses her.

"Shall we speak of questions and answer—or just make love? Contemplate or consummate? What shall it be, woman?"

Fiona, somewhat giddy from the day's wonders… and the night's questions, replies meekly.

"First, let me share the riddle of the great golden coin of Augustalis. It is rightfully tucked away in the hands of Edmud so he can do with it what he will… and I promised him that this special coin would always remain buried with him."

"Now," sneered Jason, "That is a wasted treasure."

"And what of your son, Jason, and heir to your property, pray tell?" quizzes Fiona, as she slips from her scarlet wedding gown – and stands, quite beautifully, in the autumn moonlight.

"Well," begins Jason, trying his best to stay focused. "It is a convoluted story. When I took my son in, I was told he was my son. Life was good for a while for us three. But, upon the death of his mother, the lying wench, I learned the truth. She told me, through an agonizing confession, that I was duped into thinking the child was from my seed so I would take them both into Avery Manor for safe keeping. I now look to you, Fiona, for a rightful heir to my new vast lands."

Fiona is stunned with this unexpected blurted confession. Her imagination runs wild as she fantasizes about this revealing story… and unnerving request.

If what he says is true, I would be the only rightful heir to Avery Manor…

Completeness.

The telling of secrets behind them, Jason cuts to the chase. The time is ripe to consummate his marriage to Fiona. A time for completeness.

Jason is resolute in his power of lovemaking. This evening is to be his. He has been there before… many times before… Time and time again, to be exact. Erstwhile, he has been victoriously, nay knightly, winning over the most reluctant of lovers, ladies of the day, ladies of the night.

He is now more than ready and willing to hang his loving laundry, his twists, his turns, for all and sundry to vile at. If a ghost or spirit of this old castle was watching through the "squints"-- the peepholes in the wall-- and he felt they were, or could be, he was to be good, nay best, at what he had practiced and preached through his lifetime… a lover, albeit older … but still… a lover in good standing.

Yes, tonight, their wedding night, he will woo and win over his lovely bride. His long, slim, and talented fingers, like those of a magician, begin to undo Fiona's remaining garments with the finesse that he has learned over his many years of coaxing women to bed.

Within minutes, he has deftly undone her gossamer undergarments and delicately placed them over a chair. He unhooks her necklace of expensive hyacinth stones, and slips the precious jewelry away into his breeches' pocket for safekeeping.

"Ah, Fiona, the touch of your skin, the warmth of your body, set me on fire. I need to taste you all over, taste all of your secret places."

Jason murmurs sweetly. "Remember, my dear Fiona, your words of love... courtly love. You are indeed a most intriguing... and sensuous challenge. I will wrap you in rapture. Your heart I will capture... for I do desire to kiss the fresh dew from your lips. I will set your aching and anxious heart free."

"This is what you want, is it not, Fiona?"

He begins to nibbles at her soft breasts and slowly flicks his tongue over her erect cherry red nipples.

Fiona lies motionless, determined to endure this part of the game, but finds herself both aroused and titillated. Her soft moans of pleasure betray her.

"Come to me my sweet bride, I will teach you the art of making love."

Their bodies came together, timidly at first, with Jason leading the way... and then completely, for her body was his to sample... to savor.

Life is good. Completeness... divine.

CHAPTER TWENTY-ONE

Rude Awakening.

Thunderous pounding on her door awakens Fiona from her sweet dreams. She sits up, to realize she is alone in the cold bed. Jason is missing. Gone!

As to get her bearings, she eagerly looks around the room. She is shocked to see the bedchamber in shambles, disheveled, a tousled mess! A sea of red surrounds her… for the beautiful scarlet ball gown, her wedding dress, has been deliberately, intentionally, cut into shreds, like ribbons of blood, and strewn haphazardly about the room. Panicking, she reaches under her bed pillow for her long sharp dagger, only to find the weapon missing, gone… nowhere to be found.

The raucous rapping and banging at the door continue. A frantic voice yells out.

"Come quickly, M'Lady, something terrible has happened."

Fiona hastily wraps her body in the discarded sheets from the bed throws and quickly opens the door. A servant stands there, blabbering out of control.

"The captain of the guards is in the kitchen. He is telling a most dreadful account of what took place here at midnight. Oh, M'Lady, he found Master Jason dead… in the cemetery!"

"Oh, god, no!" Fiona cries out in a voice that borders on hysteria. She quickly dons more appropriate attire- delicate cotton pantaloons and her new husband's discarded shirt of fine silk. Throwing a wool cape over her shoulder to cover this menagerie of clothing, she scurries down to the kitchen of the great castle. She hurries and scurries – reminded of just said words.

"Hurry. Come now! Emil speaks of a most horrible tale… murder in cold blood," the frightened servant manages to report in a very shaky voice.

The Story.

Emil sits huddled in a chair by the fire, his body unsteady. He holds his head in his trembling hands. Voice, low, he slowly begins to tell his grisly tale to Fiona.

"I was sole sentry last night, which is my duty and my station. I watched through the… no, no. I heard the sound of the door to your bedchamber. As it squeaked open, I rushed to see who, or what, had disturbed or bothered you. What do I see? Low and behold, your husband Jason is moving cautiously out of the room on tiptoe! Sneaking out! Since this did not seem right to me, I immediately hid in the shadows behind him… just out of sight. He made his way slowly down the shadowy passageways, and then raced out into the moonlit night."

A knot caught in Fiona's throat. "Where did Jason go?" she asked, her voice full of dread… and knowing.

Emil's, with eyes narrowing, tried to recount each and every last detail of what he had witnessed. Settling himself for the moment, he answers Fiona's question.

"Jason makes his way easily through the courtyard as if being led by the light of the full moon. I hurried to follow his silhouette. He seemed to know where he was going; he had determination in his every step. Darting between the dark shadows cast in the moonlight, he surreptitiously stole his way to the gravesides beyond the castle, to the place where the bones of Edmud and Kyla are buried."

Intuitively, Fiona's hand rises up to cover her mouth and suppress her outcry. "No! No!"

"Fiona, I am so sorry to tell you this. It seems that Jason did sneak out of the castle for a special reason. When he got to Edmud's grave, he pushed the five large stones aside... the ones that had been placed there to contain Edmud's spirits... and he started frantically digging in the mound of dirt that covers the shallow grave... with your dagger... He dug... stroke after stroke after stroke... like he knew that something of value was hidden in that soil of death."

Emil pauses, trying to catch his breath. "But then, something ghostly happens..."

Fiona goes to Emil and puts her arms around his wide shoulders in an effort to calm him and give him comfort, for he is overwhelmed by fear about what he is about to reveal.

Fiona urges him to proceed with his tale.

Gathering his thoughts, his voice, raw with fatigue and fright, Emil continues.

"Jason feverishly sifts through the dirt with his fingers. Upon finding the valuable coin, the coin of Augustalis, he hold it high in his hand and shouts into the starry night."

Jason cried out, "Ha! The priceless gold coin is mine at last... mine, mine!"

"I could not believe what happened next," Emil blurts out, and covers his eyes reliving the shear unrelenting terror of what he had witnessed in the moonlight.

"Out of Edmud's grave, liminal figures arise, the ghostly barrows and the banshees... shrieking and wailing... As the light filtered through from the fields of darkness, these spirits of the dead... scream his name... 'Jason, Jason, Jason'... seeking revenge... enveloping him in a white hazy mist, striking at him with your dagger, over and over and over... blood gushed from his throat... and then that horrible gurgling sound of death..." Emil's voice trails off.

Frightened moans escape the lips of servants listening attentively to Emil's horror story. One servant speaks up.

"I heard the eerie banshees wailing in the night, too, the scary wooing and moaning, like you said. I have heard the horrific sound of the barrows before, always calling out the name of the next to die."

"Me, too!" a second servant concurs in a voice filled with alarm.

"Once the screeching sound of the barrows enters your ears and rolls around in your head, you will never forget it. Emil is telling the truth."

"Take me to him. I must see for myself if Jason is dead," commands Fiona.

Jason is Dead.

Covered with the autumn leaves urged loose from the trees in the nearby apple orchard, the cemetery, set apart by pillars of stone, once a place of eternal rest, now lay violated and dishonored. Death is in the air.

Fiona's body freezes as she approaches. She is scarcely prepared for what she sees. Markings of evil and doom target the scene of horrific devastation: signs of digging... scarifying... plundering... Edmud's grave partially unearthed... The poignant smell of freshly dug earth, the rancid odor of dried blood and dead flesh, all combine to assail her nostrils with the vile odor of death.

Sounds abound. She can almost hear ghosts screaming out eulogies into the dawn. She is mesmerized by the horror of the sight of Jason. His face, almost unrecognizable, purple in death. Blood, running from splayed, open neck wounds, darkens the ground around him... congealing... forming a full dark red circle—a Celtic Circle—that oddly surrounds the gravesite. His mutilated body, cruelly twisted and crushed into a macabre shape, lies atop the five gravestones, He resembles the devil himself! And there, clenched in his tightly gnarled fist, is one lone golden coin. Even in death, Jason was unwilling to surrender his lustful prize.

Emil then hands Fiona a dagger, its tip, covered in red blood.

She stares at him. "My dagger?" she asks in dismay. "What is my dagger doing here?"

"I found it near the body. Jason must have stolen it from under your pillow."

"My dagger is the murder weapon?" She starred at Emil in horror, realizing the truth.

"Your new husband clearly put up a terrible fight for the coin, but the angry barrows put up an even better fight to end Jason's evil life," states Emil, putting his arm around Fiona, trying to console her in her fears.

"Gods, help me, for I do not know if I will ever be able to erase this troubled scene from my mind," Fiona sighs, taking in and letting out a long deep audible breath of sorrow.

"Fiona, prepare yourself, there is more."

Emil leads Fiona to Kyla's gravesite. Around the standing stone hangs Kyla's hyacinth necklace, sparkling in the autumn sunrays that dart though the cemetery. The sight was eerily discomforting… mocking her.

"That is the necklace you wore as a bride just yesterday, is it not?" says Emil, his eyes probing for answers.

A cry spilled past her lips. She reached out but fear took her breath.

He continues on, "The spirits may be content now as no more can be taken from them. The barrows fought back, and Jason's evil spirit lost! The spirits of Castle Baine have had their revenge with wickedness."

A look of relief crosses Fiona' face. "The spirits of Castle Baine have indeed spoken. I never doubted them… nor the labors of the gods and the spirits when they work in one's favor."

"But what are we to do now to quiet the spirits and put them to rest?" questions Emil.

Fiona responds quickly, effusive in her directions. "We will keep the spirits' ire at bay, and secure their trust. We must bury the coin of Ausgustalis in its proper place under the rocks and dirt of Edmud's grave so he will sleep in peace, once again."

"Hurry now! Time is of the essence," says Fiona, urging Emil to immediately dislodge the golden coin from Jason's tight death grip and place it at rest in the grave of its rightful owner, Edmud.

"Fiona, think for a minute. Perhaps this is not our sole recourse. Why not use the coin in our favor instead of burying it with the dead?" quizzes Emil, his eyes darkening with personal thoughts of reward.

"A promise is a promise… Boidh se." (So be it.)

To die at nighttime is probably best. The soul of man is guided by moonlight- on his journey to the hereafter. It enables one to rip the clouds apart – to display the path that must be taken. To sit on the throne quite designed for the wayward soul. Count his blessings? Count his money? And the queen sits in the parlor eating bread and honey.

Grabbing Fiona's elbow, Emil steers her back to the well-lighted castle. "Tell me you did not make love to that wicked man… that was not the plan!"

She answers only with down cast yellow eyes.

CHAPTER TWENTY-TWO

Burial of Jason Avery.

Fiona watches the gloomy courtyard scene below from the hidden massive stone tower. A chilling autumn rain had fallen adding to the dreariness of the event she espied… Jason Avery leaving Castle Baine for the last and final time. Feet first. *Thank the gods.*

She is gladdened with her thoughts. Retribution leaves a cool, sweet taste in her mouth. Yes, revenge is a wonderful dessert served cold, and the completion of this plan had taken much time and precise planning.

The hearse that transports Lord Jason Avery's bodily remains, encased in a quickly nailed together box of oak, ambles over the castle's huge wooden drawbridge. The easy gait of the horses, with their legs lifting alternately in unison, suggests a less than normal speed as it exits.

She observes the horse drawn wagon of death. Bound for somewhere, perhaps even a potter's field. A few mourners lollygag behind the black-mantled hearse as it wheels its way down the wet wheel rutted road. Fiona wished they would travel as fast as a crow flies so the Avery's remains would be completely, bag and baggage, out of her life, so serenity could settle in, and the troubled, muddied waters of Castle Baine could flow clear.

"Are they traveling unhurriedly for fear of waking the dead? Begone, evil one!"

Fiona thinks back on the macabre events of the morning. Jason's body being found, brutally beaten… and dead. The blustery autumn wind streaming Una's cloak back like the wings of a bat as she rushes to the site of the corpse where she will anointed his dead body with sweet smelling spices and perfumed oils; place death bracelets and anklets on his wrists and his feet, and chant the rites of the Sidhe, the gods of wind and flame, for protection from Jason Avery's evil threats against any and all who dwell at Castle Baine.

Upon ending the ritual, Una, pleading one final caveat, warns, "Trust no one. Not now, not ever. Importantly, remember that Jason is be buried far away from Castle Baine as the spirits of Lady Kyla and Edmud will never rest in peace until he is planted deep beneath the earth… anywhere outside of this land."

The Confrontation.

The news of Jason's Avery's death had spread like wildfire throughout the glens, bringing in its wake the inflamed son of Jason, seeking answers. He arrives with the only brave bunch of ruffians from Avery Manor whom he could muster on such short notice. The son, though showing little remorse at his father's death, vehemently orders that he be given a full account of the man's sudden and grim demise.

In Fiona's stead, Emil is well prepared to answer all questions the son might bring forth. A confrontation, a war of words between the two men, ensues in the Great Hall of Castle Baine.

Within moments, the din of the heated argument, this airing of dirty laundry, brings all and sundry within earshot. The servants, gathering outside the door of the great room like rats with raised antennae, do not miss a trick or a trickle of goodly and gory gossip.

The son, his tone belligerent, casts the first stone. "I have a right to know what events took place here that led to the death of my father," demands young Avery, in a voice that echoes rudely throughout the castle, "and I will accept no lies."

"You speak of lies? Your life is built on lies," Emil countered, turning to face his opponent. "I have learned that you have been a coddled and reckless child all your lifetime. Do you think with your glossy exterior you can hid your he'ing and she'ing, your rude eclectic manner and misspent life?"

"Look at you," Emil continues in his tough lecture, "glossed over in the clothes of a gentleman. You are neither gentleman nor soldier. Your heart is not brave- not like a true highlander. You are ne'er heroic or knightly… when all you think of is yourself."

Emil pauses, knowing the blow he is about to deliver. " Do not speak to me of lies. The truth. I will give you the truth. I will start with the first of many."

Can you handle the truth? Emil wonders.

"You are not your Jason Avery's son. We have learned otherwise. You are a bastard child—an ignoble man. You are neither the true son, nor the true heir to Avery Manor… neither kit nor kin. That valuable estate has been willed to Fiona of Castle Baine as the wife and widow of Jason Avery, the man you claim to be your father. The church itself blessed Fiona and

Jason's marriage. This is true, legally true," says the composed Emil, taking charge of the disruptive situation. He spoke with authority. The fateful stone has been cast.

A minute passes, maybe more, before the son of Jason launches his retaliatory attack. He is suddenly trembling with wrath and disbelief; face, flame red; eyes that do not smile. He tries desperately to reweave the unraveling tapestry.

"We had a pact, my father and I. He would not have told you the truth of my birth unless you beat it out of him, and, according to your servants, his body was severely and brutally trodden, almost beyond recognition," the son argues, caustically, showing off his well trained tongue.

Seemingly unperturbed by the man's tirade, Emil lowers his voice and strongly carries on.

"My words are true. You find not for your countrymen, but only for yourself— both in deceit and deception. You and Jason Avery had a voracious appetite for land. I know this, for I, too, have experienced the Avery plundering and taking away. My very own father's castle to the north once fell victim to your family's willful maundering and murder. Yes, murder. My home, ravished...burned. Without caring and thought from you... or Jason."

Instantly, the room reeks of silence. Young Avery, his face red with anger, retaliates.

"How dare you speak to me with your idle dawdle. Your lies are tantamount to slander. You foolish guard ... or is it lackey for Lady Baine?"

Emil sagaciously ignored the livid reply and leaned forward. His voice turned suddenly stern.

"Learn from the life of your "so called" father. Yes, he was a rich and powerful noble, only in his fiftieth year. But, it is the quality of life a man leads... not the quantity of age. And death is never timely. Jason was not a pious man... evil lurked in his heart... he was corrupt. He stole from all he was connected with. He betrayed both friend and foe, and broke the vows of trust. His greed was his downfall. The gods will have their revenge, it is the law of the ages," Emil decrees.

Innately aware his words fell on deaf ears, he has no remorse for the shadow of this man who calls himself, son of Jason.

Emil brings this war on words to a close, ever watching the son out of the corner of his eye.

"Be consoled by what has come to pass on this very day. Jason's body has been well made ready for burial. He was anointed, the pockets of his weskit were sown shut as not to allow any spirits to accompany him to the after world. Golden coins cover his eyes so he will not experience the baneful powers of darkness. One coin was put under his tongue to keep his body from being taken away to Hades. He has been well prepared to face the life of the hereafter."

The son turned grave. Uneasiness rolled over him, a kind of queasy fatalism. He answers stiffly.

"I will take my father and give him a rightful burial. He will be buried at the top of the hill, where the Lords of the Highlands are buried, not at the bottom with the knaves... like you are suggesting."

In harsh reality, devious thoughts ran through young Avery's mind-- a scheming look masked his face.

I will indeed find the coins... and more... and keep all for myself.

Standing, Emil folds his arms across his broad chest—his position exudes power.

"I speak for Fiona, Jason's widow. She has accepted what has transpired on this dark day. In compensation, she is prepared to pay you the sum of thirty valuable coins for the burial of his body... and in recognition of your loss."

The deal is cut. Emil gives the man the shiny golden coins, all the while thinking to himself.

"One would have thought you the son of Jason, that avaricious man, for you are the same greedy bastard."

Not knowing enough to play the smart card, leave and say nothing, young Avery has one final rebuke.

"Then let the loving wife take over the manor and let her try to put the new estate in order!" His palate savored the sweet taste of his threat.

As he storms out of the great hall, the son of Jason almost stumbles over the servants who have had their ears glued to the door, missing nary a word.

The listening rats, the tell tale rats.

Rats—see how they run.

Coins jingling, the son leaves with the body of Jason Avery, to be buried, who knows where, but rest assured, all golden coins will be missing from the anointed corpse... and missing as well, will be all valuables from Avery Manor!

Alone at Last.

Emil and Fiona are relieved that the death carriage and its somber entourage have finally departed the castle.

"I am sorely afraid that we have not seen the last of the man who calls himself Jason's son... that evil scoundrel is not to be trusted."

"Stay calm, Fiona. You know how to confront evil," Emil pontificates, still in his preaching mood.

"But I have no patience with a man like Jason's son. His looks and charm had fooled me once... but never twice. You did well bargaining with that devil on my behalf; you wore your suit of armor well."

"We need to do what needs to be done. Let us ride there on the morrow to see what Avery Manor holds for us. I want to see the Highlands through your eyes." Calmness enters the room.

"In the meantime, Fiona, learn from the evils of the past so you will be able to dominate the future... the past is your powerful weapon. Remember, you now have possession of... nay, rule over... the richest and most fertile lands from Castle Baine... to the sea. Stay the course."

She stared at Emil a long time. Paused in her thinking. Finally she shook her head. "You are right, Emil. Jason's son has no right to the Avery land. That land is truly mine... mine... and baby Miah's!"

A silent shiver slides up her spine. She cannot help thinking: *I have personally paid dearly for the land. No one will take it away! Not now... Not ever!*

First Light.

The first light of day enters and dances on the west wall of the bedchamber. The bog fire warms the room with its cozy glow. They are cuddled beneath the covers like two spoons in a drawer.

"I have waited patiently for this time to arrive, dear 'mistress of the castle'," he whispers into her soft brown hair.

"It is time to un-steel your heart and return mine to me-- the heart you unknowingly stole that wonderful morning in the meadow... the day we made a vow to each other... when our love was magic... and needed no witch's brew."

Within the arms of Emil's gentle caress, Fiona stirs. A warm smile is on her face, as she remembers the meadow—from whence they had watched the free birds fly... the day they had first made love... and made their future plans... together.

She traces the small "t" birthmark on his rugged shoulder with nimble fingertips. She clings to him tightly, trusting that he will never leave her.

"Do you have enough land and castles?" Emil queries.

She watches a faint smile cross his face, never having taken her eyes from him.

"That, Emil my love, is a very silly question. And why do you ask, pray tell?" She pouted lusciously.

"I ask, simply because... Castle Moorehaven, with its beautiful orchards and farmland, just meters to the south, has a Lord that is very, very, lonely."

She portrays the ingénue, a role she has perfected, immediately donning her "acting" face!

In reality, she knows that Lord Moorehaven is truly lonely for she has already put into motion plans to befriend him, get to know him on a deep personal level, comfort him… she, the kind and loving neighbor, the Lady of Castle Baine. At that moment, an unexplained breeze enters the closed room. Or was it the beating of Emil's heart?

With a theatrical flair, Fiona, abandoning the fur-lined covers, dramatically says to Emil, "Come with me, M'Lord, my angel." A soft playful sounding laugh slipped past her lips.

"Let us feast on sweet-spiced apples and haggis… before we ride out to survey the land… our land. Come, let us dance in the forest… and play in the fields."

The fog is lifting from the scene where the waters of the mighty Knell flow; the pale moon rises above the green lands—the mountains and the glens. It is time for happiness again. A time for safe sailing. For the chosen one-- the tides have turned. Biodh se.

ABOUT THE AUTHOR

The authors present an intriguing, fast moving fantasy of medieval castle life in the Highlands of Eire.

Mirror twins…identical, one an intellect, with a Ph.D. Right-handed … winner of awards, from teacher… to Alumni of the year. The other, left-handed, a feisty tennis player with killer instincts… winner of poetic tribute… Both early writers of macabre short stories.

And herein lies the rub… they defy you to differentiate between the places where one begins the sentence and the other ends it! Who is dotting the i's? Who crossed the t's? Be aware, born under the sign of Scorpio… both love the touch of the unknown and all secrets hidden within… They bring bizarre twists and magical wit to their writing.

Printed in the United States
33395LVS00011B/70-87

9 781420 830439